POTPOURRI

A Mixture of Short Stories, Flash Fiction and Poetry

John Corral

ISBN-13: 9798760561190
ISBN-10: 1477123456

Cover design by: Art Painter
Library of Congress Control Number: 2018675309
Printed in the United States of America

*To my dear sister Jovita. Thank you for a lifetime
of generosity, understanding and love.*

That it will never come again is what makes life sweet. Dwell in possibility. Find ecstasy in life; the mere sense of living is joy enough.

EMILY DICKINSON

CONTENTS

PREFACE

This is a collection of short stories, flash fiction and poetry, that, like potpourri, is a mixture of different things, scented and spiced. They are here, as in a bowl, placed to provide the reader with small samples of the ordinary anxieties and passions of life. In this collection you will meet kings and paupers, dreamers and devils, the young and the not so young. They appear in a great variety of interesting pieces that, in the end, are life-affirming and heart-warming, most with some funny twists.

Three of the these poems have been made available previously in poem collections by this author on Amazon.

THE BOX

One day Gerald got a phone call that changed his life. It was from an attorney in Albuquerque, who asked him some questions about his background, and then told him that the attorney was the executor of his father's estate. Gerald slammed the phone down. The attorney called back, but he didn't answer. He called several more times before leaving a message. Gerald deleted it. He left similar messages over the next few days, which were also removed.

A week later, Gerald received a letter from the attorney. He tore it up. The next week Gerald received another letter, which he also tore up. After more phone calls and several letters later, the attorney turned up at Gerald's front door. He expected that and didn't answer the doorbell, nor the knocks at the door. The attorney left and returned the next day. The same things occurred.

Two weeks passed, and Gerald received a large box with no return address on it. He knew it was from the attorney. His first inclination was to burn it, but he didn't. The box sat his desk for over a week before he opened it and read the letter inside. It said the following:

Mr. Gerald Burns,

Let me first offer my deepest condolences for your loss. Your father *died recently, and I am entrusted to carry out the final distribution to the heirs of his estate. Enclosed, please find a cashiers check in the amount of $313,540. This sum is payable to you for your proportionate share of the estate.*

Please note that the estate assets were liquidated and distributed to the persons entitled to receive them according to New Mexico state laws of succession. There was no will. However, in that event, what was done was in accordance with New Mexico state law governing such matters. Attached please find a copy of the statute for your review on this. Also attached is a complete accounting of the assets, debts, costs, and fees. Taxes on distributions are your responsibility. Please check with your tax advisor on this.

Sincerely,

Mortimer J. Reynaldo, Esq.

As the letter mentioned, a check was stapled for the amount specified. Gerald had never had anything close to that amount of money, ever. Almost a quarter of a million dollars. But seeing that check made him sick to his stomach. He wanted to tear up the check, or burn it, or bury it somewhere. Why? His father had left him, his sister, and his mother to run off with another woman, and never saw them again. Gerald was six then, and now he was 54.

He knew something like this would happen. He was contacted when his father died last Spring, but Gerald refused to go to his father's funeral. His half-brother called, someone he didn't know existed until he introduced himself. It wasn't a cordial conversation. And he never called back. His half-brother was the only living relative from that union, and since Gerald's sister died a few months after his mother passed away a few years ago, Gerald was the only one left from his family. Gerald was married once and had a girl, but his wife and his daughter were killed in a car crash some years before.

Gerald stared at the box. It was large and held other things, papers mostly, pictures, and a few odds and ends such as baseball cards and picture postcards. He didn't want to see them. I closed up the box. He was tempted to burn it all, sight unseen. He took it out of the house and put it near the trash bins.

Dale, his half-brother's name, told Gerald a few things about his father before the shouting began and hung up the phone. He said he never knew his father had another family, which he left behind when he and his mother came to Santa Fe where her family was from. She was an artist, one-quarter Navajo, and had a small gallery there. His father had always wanted to paint, and with her help, he developed a style that sold fairly well, and they had a successful business until she died about ten years ago. They never married officially, but they went through a Navajo ceremony that was recognized in that state. When Gerald declared that bigamy is when Dale got angry. And Gerald said some other things like, "So he was an adulterer instead, which is probably worse." They exchanged quite a few ugly words after that.

Gerald didn't remember his dad; how he looked or what he was like. His mother threw out all his pictures. And nobody in her family, or even in town, mentioned his name after he left. It was like he never existed. When Gerald was asked to fill in his father's name at school, he always left it blank. When others in town didn't see he was around, they might mention his father and talk about him. Gerald learned that he was a salesman in a department store, and that's where he met the woman he ran off with. He was said to be a popular guy, a good worker, handsome, polite, and a good athlete. In high school, he had lettered in two sports, baseball and track. That's why Gerald avoided sports, and instead concentrated on music. He played the violin, sang in glee, and performed every show the high school put on in his last two years.

Gerald's sister never knew him. She was two when he left. But she missed him the most. Not Gerald's mother. She never spoke about him, even when Gerald's sister begged her to. It was said Gerald's sister looked most like him with her green eyes, pale skin, and reddish-blond hair. But that was all he left her. Gerald's mom had taken everything that she identified with him and threw it all away. He had taken only a few clothes with him. Everything else, most of his clothes, his books, his sports things, even his hunting rifle, she threw into the river outside of town. Gerald was with her when she did that, helping her to carry items. She flung them over the side, they heard the splash, and then she crumbled to the ground and cried. She got up a few minutes later, and never talked about him again.

The large box with his things remained outside for almost a month. Gerald brought it in and put it in the basement where it stayed for nearly a year. Still, he thought about it almost every day. Finally, Gerald brought it up to his living room and opened it again. Then he started looking through it.

The top layer were things associated with his life in Santa Fe. There were lots of pictures of people Gerald didn't recognize. Most were Indians because of their dark skin, though he couldn't tell. Nothing from his former life. No pictures of Gerald, his sister, or his mother. It was like his previous life never existed. He wasn't a father to Gerald or his sister. He was a blank. Like Gerald thought.

In the second layer, there were some books on art and a Bible. He had been married to Gerald's mother in the First Baptist Church right in town. As a tradition, they give the newly married couple a Bible with their names inscribed. Gerald looked at the front cover, and there were his father's name and the name of his mother. Funny, he had kept that. He left her to run away with another woman, but he kept the Bible that had this inscription: Joseph and Emily Burns, Husband and Wife Forever.

Gerald sat down and cried. He felt weak after that and left the box for the next day. But he thought about it: what possessed him to keep that Bible all those years? Had the new woman in his life ever questioned him about it? What did she know about him before they ran away together? That he was married and had small children to support? And how would the family survive? Did she or he ever wonder about that?

As it happened, Gerald's mother's family was quite supportive. And they lived in a few places, settling down after a few years with a widowed aunt. The people at the church were generous and helped out with clothes and food occasionally. And after Gerald's mother got a job waiting tables, that helped. But it was hard, very hard for a few years.

The third layer in the box were the things Gerald dreaded. Letters, hundreds of them. He didn't want to read them, but he did. They were his father's letters, addressed to her, the new woman in his life. Love letters. And they were in cursive writing, in black ink as from a fountain pen, beautifully done, almost works of art. Gerald glanced at them and noted words like "dear" "angel" "darling" and "adored." Again, that made him nauseous. He cringed. He wept. But he read them. They were written while he was away from her, probably at art shows or festivals because he would say, "Dearest one, I am not with you, but I left my heart there. Take hold of it, and adore it, as you have taken the whole of me." And, "I am yours forever, as you are mine forever, til our ashes mingle in the desert wind."

Gerald spent the rest of that night and the next going over every letter. His father was a loving man who had found someone he had loved dearly. Gerald could see that. But it was crushing to him that he could be so loving toward her, and not towards him. Then he found a picture of them. The only one in the box. It was taken with them dressed in Indian paraphernalia. They were somber-faced. And they looked young and innocent.

Then Gerald found a framed poem. It was in his father's cursive writing, and probably written by him. It read:

Santa Fe

When I last left my Santa Fe,
The desert heat reigned in the day.
The desert wind blew far and free,
Beneath the blue of the big sky sea.

Oh! -- To finally say,
I'm back at home,
In my Santa Fe.

I have scaled many mountains bare,
And breathed in the most exotic air.
I have conquered all I did survey,
For a hundred months and a day.

But, oh! -- To finally say,
I'm back at home,
In my Santa Fe.

But I've been fretful each night I lie,
And watched the dark eternal sky,
Counting the stars as they turn and spin,
That drew me closer to the world I'm in.

Oh! -- To finally say,
I'm back at home,
In my Santa Fe.

I could hear the desert song,
That repeats, repeats all night long,
The song went on loud and clear.

And, oh! -- To finally say,
I'm back at home,
In my Santa Fe

When I finally returned to my Santa Fe,
At long last one fine day,

There arose in me a wistful sigh,
As white clouds billowed in the sky.

Oh! -- To finally say,
I'm back at home,
In my Santa Fe.
I'm back at home,
--And home I'll stay!

Gerald didn't know what to make of it. Was that a love poem to her or to the life he had there in Santa Fe? Was that what drew him to that place and her? Gerald would never know the answer to that question. He decided to burn everything after that. Everything. Even the check. What would he do with the money? He had what he needed, and anything else wasn't going to make him any happier. He had his memories of his wife and child, and he knew he had taken care of them as he should have.

As to his father, he was not going to judge him. God had done that already. And he was not going to have any further contact with his half brother. His memories were not Gerald's, and Gerald's were not his. He would not think of him or his father anymore. When his father left Gerald behind, he gave up his right to be thought of by him.

As he set fire to the box, Gerald thought, *I have many memories of my sister, my mother, my wife, and my child. They are happy memories, and that's all I have time for.*

MARION AND CECIL

It was the third Sunday in August, and Marion Turner wasn't looking forward to the next day's drive and the next full week that she and her husband Cecil would spend in Pah Tempe Hot Springs in the deep river canyon that bisects Hurricane and LaVerkin, Utah. It was only a three-hour drive, but Cecil seldom drove anymore, except to town with her once a week for groceries and other supplies, and to Church on Sundays. They had been going to Pah Tempe since their kids were still in school, and both Raymond and Jessica were in their forties now and had kids of their own. Cecil was 78 now and not a youthful 78 like Marion's brother Jessie, more like cousin Eleanor, who had health problems all her life and died at 63.

They were expecting Summer thunderstorms the next day to Pah Tempe, and Cecil didn't like to drive in the rain. His eyesight was poor, and their '86 Dodge Caravan had over 163,000 miles on it. He usually took it each year to have it checked out by Tom the mechanic at the Shell Station before each trip, but Tom's been out lately. They say cancer because someone at church said they saw Tom spitting blood, but nobody knows for sure. And if the car wasn't something to worry about, they also had Nancy, their cat who had to be taken to the Vet because she was acting sluggish lately. He didn't found anything but said to "watch her and let me know if she has problems walking or leaking, or anything else unusual." Nancy was going on 15, and older than Whiskers was when he had to be put down.

Marion always had her eyes go moist when she remembered Whiskers, her favorite of the cats they had. And she remembered him now in worrying about Nancy. Marion always went over her worries at night before going to sleep. She and Cecil would get into bed, turn on the TV to the ten o'clock news out of Cedar Creek, and he would comment on the news while she stared at the TV, but thought about other things. Cecil would usually turn off the TV and fall asleep before she was through worrying.

Marion was first up, as she usually was, and fixed the coffee. She'd make extra this morning so they could take a thermos to sip along the way. She always did, but Cecil never had any. Still, he might this time. Or he'd ask her why she didn't if she hadn't brought a thermos. Cecil was like that. Always finding something to complain about, and never finding anything satisfactory. She had finished packing a week before so he could tell her what she had missed. Was it the new leather jacket he wanted to take, or would the old flannel one do? And how about his underwear? One extra set or two? No matter her guesses, she was always wrong.

Marion wore her newest dress, the green one that she got for their granddaughter's graduation from high school. Would Cecil notice? He never commented on how she dressed or noticed anything new she wore. But it was ten exactly when Cecil started up the car, and he wanted her to notice that. That was something he always did with the words, "By Jiminy, right on time!"

He got on Interstate 15 after going through town and headed south at fifty-five miles an hour, hugging the right side of the road, and clutching the wheel at the ten and two positions. He seldom said anything to her while driving. But he did mumble things under his breath like "He's an idiot" when a semi would blast past him. Or, say, "Can't he see I'm at the posted speed limit?" When a driver would honk his horn. Cecil would sometimes call out what the billboards said, something his father did with Burma Shave signs. And he'd use the same words as his dad, "That's a knee slapper," or "That's a dandy."

They usually got to Fillmore by eleven, and then Cedar City by noon to get lunch there. But not this day since they got rained on several times by thunderstorms and had to drive very slowly, down to thirty at times. It was twelve-thirty, and Cecil's stomach was grumbling. A turn-off was coming up, and a sign said a Denny's was there. Cecil looked over at Marion and said, "Want to stop for lunch?"

Marion had been thinking about Whiskers and said, "If it were up to me, I'd just as soon turn around and go home."

It was the wrong thing to say. With Cecil hungry, it was the very worse thing she could say. And something snapped inside of him. Maybe it had been festering for some time, just waiting for a moment like this, because he stopped by the side of the road, slapped the seat space between them hard, and said, "Well, of course, I'm sure you want to go back home. Never mind that I'm hungry and need to eat. You don't care. You never care about me one little bit, and you never have. So it's not surprising that you don't care now. You don't care if I live or die. You'd probably just as soon see me dead so that I wouldn't bother you none anymore by getting on top of you once a month. That'd make you happy, wouldn't it? You'd clap your hands. You'd go out and celebrate with Christine. Because you'd be free of me, wouldn't you? No more fixing me food, or washing my clothes, or any of the woman chores. Well, you ain't no good at woman chores, and never have been. That's what Ma said years ago, and she was right!"

Marion stared at Cecil. Did she really hear him say those words? Tears came to her eyes. She blew her nose. This is how he felt after nearly fifty years of marriage? Then she said, "I would care if you died."

"Oh yeah, how much? You tell me!"

Marion wasn't good with theoretical questions. After a couple of minutes, she said, "Well, I guess if you don't know by now, I can't convince you that I do. The Bible says, 'the great things are those in plain sight,' but you have to figure out what they are. That's Proverbs 33:3."

Cecil thought for a moment, hard, and then said, "No, that's Jeremiah 33:3."

Marion said, "I love you, Cecil, and that's the truth. And you have to know that."

Just then, the sun broke through the clouds, and they were in bright sunlight. Cecil looked at Marion and could see tears in her eyes. And tears came to his eyes. He'd never heard her say she loved him, nor had he ever said those words to her. He loved her; he knew that. And he wanted to say those words now, but he couldn't. It occurred to him that she might leave him on account of his stubbornness. That was plain dumb, but he had his pride. There wasn't time to think this through clearly. He took her hand and squeezed it, saying, "I'm sorry about what I said. I don't know what got into me. I promise never to say such stupid things again."

Marion was quiet for a moment. She closed her eyes, then opened them and said, "What stupid things? I think I dozed off for a while and woke when the sun appeared. Look, there's a Denny's up ahead. I wonder if they still have the chicken-fried steak on the menu that you like?"

POEMS: THE PATH; REALITY; OUR LIVES

The Path

There was a road once
That seemed like it was my path.
I could feel it pull me,
But I pulled as hard right back.

I know I can't return now,
That road was made of sand,
It disappeared with a strong wind
That blew in from my past.

Reality

On his break, the messenger of reality speaks:

"I don't like my job and no one likes me.
I don't have wings like the spirit of dreams
or a halo like the hero of happiness.
No, I have nothing but this old broom
and a trash can. So it is my doom
to see everyday the dirt of society.
I am reality."

"I am everywhere. I mostly stand
doing what I can dealing with the needs
and the demands of life.
I am not glamorous, nor charismatic.
No poems are written about me.
No one has me as their shining star.
I am reality."

"But I am life, true life.
Everything else is not.
And I am everything they cannot
say they ever were, are, or can be.
Accept it. I have. It is a certainty.
And believe what things I've taught.
I am reality."

Our Lives

We live the story of our lives
As if we're reading from a book.
Each page is a day that comes;

Each chapter ends as we take a look.

There is no other author here;
It is only us that write the tale:
Our lives unfold the way we want:
Recording us to win, or pen the words to fail.

WHEN ERNEST IS KING

In high school, Ernest Voit was in Thespians, the school's drama club, and Glee Club. He wasn't very good in those and never starred in any plays or musicals that the high school staged each year. A smallish boy, he lacked the good looks and charisma that were keys to success in the performance arts. He also couldn't sing that well. But he was a dreamer.

At the talent show, he did magic tricks using playing cards one year and came in third. The next year he told jokes and got some chuckles, but didn't place in the top three. And in his senior year, he did impressions of famous people. The trouble is, he chose obscure celebrities from the Golden Age of Hollywood —Jimmy Stewart, Henry Fonda, and Humphrey Bogart, and few in the audience knew them. He was laughed off the stage.

Ernest was never encouraged by his parents. They were both quiet and sensible people. His father worked as an auto mechanic, and his mother worked as a waitress at one of the diners in town. The couple had four children, and Ernest was the oldest. The second oldest was his sister Marie, who was two years younger, and the twin girls were five years younger than Marie.

Life had not been easy for the Voit family. When Ernest was ten, his father, Thomas, came down with TB and was out of work for six months. He had to leave his good-paying job with the telephone company and only held part-time jobs afterward until someone from the church hired him. His mother was a teller at one of the banks. But the manager didn't want to take the chance she might be infected and pass it on to one of the customers. She lost her job and could only get part-time jobs after that, mostly in back rooms somewhere as a clerk. And after missing a few payments on the small house they were buying, the couple had to move into a mobile home.

It was hard living in a mobile home, which was the size of their former living room. When everyone else was asleep, Ernest would close his eyes and wish for the life he wanted. He would mouth the words of a poem by Milne:

I often wish I were a King,
And then I could do anything.

If only I were King of Spain,
I'd take my hat off in the rain.

If only I were King of France,
I wouldn't brush my hair for aunts.

I think if I were King of Greece,
I'd push things off the mantelpiece.

If I were King of Norroway,
I'd ask an elephant to stay.

If I were King of Babylon,
I'd leave my button gloves undone.

If I were King of Timbuctoo,
I'd think of lovely things to do.

If I were King of anything,
I'd tell the soldiers, "I'm the King!"

And that would make him feel better. It was his grandfather who taught him that poem. "Someday, you will be king," his grandfather told him. "It's only a matter of time."

His grandfather, who was also a dreamer, told Ernest, "What will you do as king? This is what you have to concern yourself with, not whether it will happen. Will you marry a princess and make her a queen? Will you build a big castle? Or will you find a big, beautiful castle somewhere and make it yours? Will it have a moat and high walls? A crystal chandelier in the great hall? Fireplaces everywhere, even in the bedrooms? Oriental rugs on all the floors, oil paintings, and tapestries on the walls? And will you have a beautiful white horse to ride through your kingdom so that your subjects could bow before you?"

His family knew all about what Ernest dreamed of. They had simple tastes and didn't wish for those things. But they never discouraged Ernest from dreaming big. And if Ernest asked them, they would tell him what they wanted. "When I am king, what wishes do I grant you?" He'd say. His sister Anne wanted a pony; the twins wanted candy, lots of chocolate candy, and his parents said they would be happy to be back in the small home they had at one time.

One day they got a letter from overseas from a place no one had heard of. Ernest even got a world atlas out and couldn't find it. The letter was addressed to Ernest, and it stated on the envelope: To Be Read Only By Ernest Voit.

Ernest took the letter outside, opened the envelope, and read the following:

"Your Royal Highness, King Ernest,

I wish to inform you that you have been identified as the true sovereign king of the country of Vouilet. This might be surprising to you, as it was to the undersigned, but let me assure you that this is true and fac-tual. Our previous king died almost a year ago without leaving an heir. Since then, extensive research has been done to determine the succes-sor. That research, preliminarily, had determined that you, through a branch of the family that governed the kingdom many years ago before that ancestor left the kingdom to emigrate to America several hundred years ago, are now the rightful king. We know your birth father died some years ago, and that your mother remarried the person that you know as your father now."

The letter went on to say how the succession was determined, noting names and dates of birth, through a long series of princes, counts, earls, and marquises, until it got to the person who was the birth father of Ernest. It also detailed how other possible succession lines had been found to be extinct, thus making Ernest the exclusive heir to the throne of Vouilet.

It also provided information on where the kingdom was located. It was a tiny country, only a few square miles, and had only a population of several thousand people. It lay close to the present border between France and Germany to its east. It was bounded by an old Roman road that ran from Poitiers to Nantote to the south, had the river Auzance as its northern boundary, and ended at the forest edge of Sandes for its west border. Also, it provided, at the bottom, this warning:

"Now, for the difficult part. You must not tell anyone of this. Forces are working against your ascension to the throne, and your life would be in danger if they learned of your whereabouts before everything is done to secure and finalize your transition to the throne. As soon as it is safe and secure to do so, I will contact you again. Then, and only then, can you tell the world of your kingship, and take your rightful place on the throne of Vouilet."

"Again, you must tell anyone! Not even your family. I will be in touch when disclosure to the world is possible. That may take years, but that day will come. Until then, I am your loyal servant,

Andre Pitot-Vienne"

Ernest was astounded beyond words. He was king! And he would rule as king someday soon. He reread the letter several times. It was too good to be true, but it was true. He was king!

Would he chance to tell anyone? He had no close friends to confide in. The kids at school would only laugh if he told them. His family? The letter said they should not be told. What about his grandfather? If he were alive, Ernest might tell him. But his grandfather died a few days before, and his funeral had been the previous week. No one must be told. Ernest would keep the letter confidential.

And Ernest never told anyone. Through many weeks, months, and years, Ernest kept the letter and what it said confidential. Yet no other letter arrived, nor any further contact by anyone about the kingship. Still, Ernest said nothing to anyone about the letter. Life went on. The family continued living in the same dismal place, doing virtually the same things. And Ernest would ask them what they wished for, "If I were King." And they gave essentially the same answers. Nothing had changed for them.

But Ernest changed. He was a different person, more confident, focused, and sure of himself. And he went to the local community college, got an AA in management and accounting, to prepare himself for his kingship. After that, he took a job at a local factory where he excelled. Years passed. Ernest married, had two children, but he never disclosed anything to anyone about the letter. He did, though, become the plant manager, and after the factory owner died, he bought the factory that was the primary employer for the town.

Did Ernest become a king? Many people in the town thought he was because he ran the factory benevolently as a good king might. And he saw to it that his parents had a house soon after he started doing well at the factory. His siblings also got their wishes fulfilled. He paid for his sister's wedding and saw that she rode in on a golden pony to be wed. The twins were also married, and they got wedding receptions that featured chocolate in every way possible.

Some years after that, Ernest decided to find out if the letter was legitimate. He hired an investigator who reported to him after a few weeks that it was mostly accurate in what it said. But with a twist. The letter had originated in Vouilet, that was true. But it was done by a retired teacher in the town of Vouilet, at the request of Ernest's grandfather. Vouilet had been a kingdom at one time, but it was now a part of France and had been for almost six hundred years.

When it was a sovereign kingdom, its king died in battle and left no apparent heirs. The people of Voiilet then pledged allegiance to the king that defeated their king in battle. Ernest's grandfather had learned that years before, after he began tracing his ancestry. He took an interest in Genealogy, did the family tree, which formed the basis for the letter and found that Ernest was the descendant to the person who had been a successor to the crown. That is, if a valid search was done at the time. The kingdom was given to another king instead. Ernest was a king, but with no kingdom… At least not in France. In his town, Ernest was king. And it was his grandfather who gave him that crown.

JEROME GETS THE VIRUS

Our town of Jerome sits near the top of Cleopatra Hill, high above Cottonwood Valley, midway between Prescott and Flagstaff, Arizona. Even by Arizona standards, it is "the sticks," and looked down on by the folks in the communities below of Clarksdale, Perkinsville, and Cottonwood. Once a thriving mining town with a population of close to 15,000 people, third largest in the state in the 1920's, we barely topped 300 in the last census.

Jerome clings to the hillside, literally in some places since the structures are narrow and built at a slant, and maintains itself as a tourist attraction for visitors because it was known as the "Wickedest Town in the West," during its heyday as one of the most productive copper mines of Phelps Dodge.

But the mine played out in the 1950's. We have historical status, officially, because it was designated a National Historic District by the federal government. About half of the buildings are opened for tourists during the Summer months, and the town gets upwards of 30,000 visitors per month according to the Visitors Bureau. But after Summer, the town is lucky to see 100 visitors per week.

Residents wear what tourists expect: well-worn jeans, raw cotton shirts in earth colors, bandanas, Stetsons, and high-heeled boots. And in keeping with our appearance, we speak in Arizona twang, and use words like "Howdy" and "Yawl come back now, y'hear?" Not that there is too much to see once you look through one or two of the buildings—simply more of the same rickety, weather-worn wooden structures that defy the weather and gravity. Most of the structures have two levels. And whether the lower floor was a general store or saloon —and a barber shop or beauty salon now, the upper story was invariable a whore house at one time, with fully half or more of the residents of the town involved in that trade.

At an elevation of 5,066 feet, Jerome experiences the four seasons unlike most of Arizona. And Winters can be harsh. The hillsides and passes get studded with snow, the frigid wind never stops, and after a partial thaw, the streets and walkways which are mostly unpaved, turn from their usual dusty, mineral-rich dirt to thick mud.

The winter of 2020 was one of the harshest. Our first snow storm was in November, and we had three times the usual snowfall during the season by most people's recollections. Already the old-timers are readying their stories: "That winter of 2020, boy, that was a bad one." "Yeah, it surely was." "Plenty of snow and ice and sleet and mud." "You couldn't go nowhere, no how." "We wuz all sick, from March to July." "It almost killed us."

Yes, the Corona Virus hit Jerome hard.

Many, *many* people got sick in Jerome, and it happened very quickly. We started hearing about the Corona Virus in early February, and by mid-March it seemed like half the town had it. Je-rome's people are hardy, salt-of-the-earth type and seldom see a doctor. Since there isn't one in town, the nearest is in Cottonwood, almost an hour's drive away, we have to tough things out.

The person everyone see for ailments is the Postmistress, Janet, a gaunt woman who wears a rawhide dress and cowboy boots, and presides over her herbal medicine store and Post Office at the end of Main St. Her place has peeling paint and is falling apart, but nobody minds that. And it loses something, a shingle or a door knob that falls down the hill daily. Janet wills her place to stay put and upright, and it does somehow. That and the place next door —Darla's Cafe, where Miss Darla, as everyone calls her, dispenses sandwiches, coffee, soft drinks, and near beer (she doesn't have a beer license), are the two centers of town.

Janet's prescription for the virus? "Live with it. Go on about your business. It'll pass and you'll get better. Or you won't. Either way, it's no use fussin' about it." And that suited most people. Janet said we'd been through the Swine Flu and the Asian Flu, and we got through those okay. And she'd heard about all the people that got through the Spanish Flu all right. Rugged hardiness is a part of life in Jerome. You could be cold, wet, and sick to your stomach, but you carried on. Misery was common, and if everything was alright, just wait. Things'll get worse soon enough.

But lots of people started coming down with the virus. The high school basketball team had nine player and four of them got it. They said it was like they normally feel before a game: feverish with cold chills, nauseous, and lethargic. The boys all felt well the day before, and by afternoon of the next day, they said they were so bad they couldn't even handle the ball. So they said they couldn't make the trip to the State tournament.

The coach got on them for being unwilling to play. "This is a test for you. Be strong. And manly. And step up when it counts. This'll shape the rest of your life. Will you answer the call? Or will you be a pussy?"

When the bus arrived, all the players got on, sick or not. The team still had five players that could suit up and the team seemed to be okay. Then the assistant coach got sick on the way there. And the next day —the day of the tournament, the head coach came down with the virus, along with two other players. In the end, it didn't matter because the tournament was canceled by the AIA because of the virus.

On the long way home, almost everyone had symptoms. It was a busload of very sick players, coaches and even some of their most fanatic supporters on an overheated bus with bad suspension swaying back and forth barreling sixty-five mph down the bumpy desert highway from Yuma, along the back way, through Sedona, that was a journey of six hours of hell, with vomiting and worse, that those folks will remember for years.

In Jerome, Harold Minor who runs the only gas station in town got sick and had to close his station for almost two weeks. Marie Pence and her two dogs became sick, and she had the only dry cleaners in town. The two general stores had limited hours because they had absent employees. So did the bank, the liquor store, the pet store, and two of the three restaurants in town. One, Gino's Pizza, closed down permanently because Gino died.

And other people died. Many of them. Seth and his wife Marilyn, both in their eighties, packed it in. They were found lying side by side in their living room, holding hands, which was touching. But they were surrounded by vomit and soiled in their diarrhea, which wasn't so nice. That was the thing with this virus that was new. Normally, if one person got sick, the other would take care of them. We're mostly couples up here, in our Seventies or older, and situations where both husband and wife got sick just didn't happen much. It's one thing to take care of a loved one, which is the right thing to do. But there aren't that many helpful, good Christian people to take care of so many others that aren't kin.

The widow McKenna came down with the flu after she tried to help out her twins, Sid and Steve. But then she got sick. So did Tracy, the widow McKenna's neighbor. Tracy's son had to drive in and take her down to the Valley to his place in Perkinsville. Then the school had to close because the teacher, Miss Reynolds, got sick. And she was out from early April to May. They closed the school, of course, and no telling when it will start up again.

What is unusual is that neither Father William or the rabbi became sick. Maybe there is a God after all? Still, Father William closed down the church, so effectively, maybe not. The reason why he closed the church was so he could tend to those that were ill or had died, which required services as well. In one very unusual event, something I've never seen happened, several families got together and had a group burial service. That's right. It was outdoors, near the cemetery, so people wouldn't have to go too far since many of them were sick. Three were in caskets and five had been cremated.

Father William's sermon that day was especially memorable. I'll always remember what he said that day, which, as best I can recall, was something like this:

"We have talked about who we are remembering here today, who they were in life, and what they meant to us. Now I want to say something about Jerome. I first set eyes on the town almost thirty years ago. I was in the Valley below and the sun was going down. I looked up and saw Jerome with beams of light engulfing it while the valley below was in near darkness. It was magnificent! And I knew I was blessed to be coming here. It had a sordid reputation, but God wanted me here, and here I would be.

Jerome was my first parish assignment, and it has remained my one and only parish because I never want to leave. Why is that? I described my first view of Jerome one night several days ago, as I were sitting by the bedside of someone we are remembering here today. That person turned to me, and asked: "Father William, where does God want me go?"

I responded, "Does it matter? You are with God, and you go wherever He wants you to go." I told him that I took that teaching from Abraham when he was called to go to a place where he would receive an inheritance. He did so, and we are told, "He went out, not knowing whither he went." That is from Hebrews 11:8.

That is the way it should be with any person who has heard the call of God, and gone with Him. Wherever you go, He is with you. And that place will be special because of that."

Father William then finished with his usual words about someday there is going to be a reunion in the sky, where there will be no more farewells, etc. Then the faithful shuffled up to the universal urn where all the ashes of the departed who had been cremated had been mingled. He dipped his thumb in the bowl of ashes and put the black smudge on their forehead and said the words God said when He threw out Adam and Eve from Paradise, "Dust thous art and unto dis thou shalt return."

Just then the hillside clouded over and within minutes the last of the season's storm provided a light snowfall. At least on this day, no rays of sunlight would be seen at sunset.

POEMS: IN THE ER;
TWO SUNSETS;
STEP UP

In the ER

A mother clutches tightly
a McDonald's Happy Meal.
Was it bought before or after
the big truck's crunching wheel?

An old man is weeping
sitting on a red plastic chair.
He didn't live the life he wanted;
now that his life's over, he's in despair.

A young girl sits crying,
with her father who cries too.
Not for themselves, but for her,
who got sick, looking after the two.

Doctors in designer sneakers
pass too quickly without looking.
They might see too much, too soon.
And that they don't look is disquieting

A man is finally relieved and happy,
until he thinks, how am I going to pay?
His mother has spent weeks in the hospital.
Being sick takes a mighty high toll, either way.

Two Sunsets

I send your way two sunsets,
as my gift to you;
One that ended a perfect day,
with a perfect view.
The second was the brightest,
because it featured stars,
that seemed to spin around the spot
where Venus visits Mars.

You may have these sunsets,
That I saved in my memory;
No one else can see these scenes,
They are only for you and me.

Step Up

Step up to middle-age,
It is finally with us now.
We all arrive at middle-age,
Though some don't know how.
We all arrive at middle-age;
Except, of course,
Those that never turn that page.

Step up to middle-age,
It is a time for planning,
When we all give and greed,
And we count all days remaining.

We all give and greed;
But, should never confuse,
Real need from the evil greed.

Step up to middle-age,
It is when the light is the brightest;
When our appetite's the best,
And when our dreams are clearest.

Yes, our appetite's the best,
The result of many years,
When hunger was not addressed.

FLYING POSSUM PIE

You start with roadkill, no older than six hours old. Older than that and it can kill you, I heard. The widow Jones cooked it once after it had blossomed out, which means it was well past a day being out in the hot sun, and she got sick... Didn't die, but she'd wished she had and told everyone so. Anyway, you scrape off anything that looks bad —head, tail, fur, and bones, and you cut up what's left. You put it in a boiling pot, cook it with potatoes, beets, and some squash. Season it with salt and pepper. Put it on medium boil and leave it for an hour. Taste it. It tastes like chicken, don't it?

No, that ain't Flying Possum Pie. Here's the real story:

It was my dad who invented Flying Possum Pie. It was back when he was courting my mom. She was a real beauty, everyone said so, and all the guys in high school were interested in her. But he wasn't much to look at, or had any real prospects of amounting to much. Still, he did surprising things so often that my mom couldn't help but keep an eye on him for that reason alone. She dated some of the "big guys on campus," but she married dad in the end. Why? Because of Flying Possum Pie.

Let me take you all the way back to the beginning. It started when they were young. My mom and dad, Jennifer and Bob, grew up together, on Hoover St, over on the West side of town, near the churches, and two blocks from the high school. They liked each other as children, had fun playing together, and thought they would always be together because, at age nine, they promised each other that they would get married when they graduated from high school. But by age ten, things changed.

She started doing "girl things" with other girls in the neighborhood, and he started hanging out with boys doing "guy things." At age thirteen, things changed again. Puberty kicked in.

She developed curves almost overnight and could no longer wear the clothes she had from the year before. Instead, she was wearing clothes that her mother had worn back when she was a young woman. And the next year, when she entered high school, she had the attention of all the boys, even the seniors. By then, she was a leggy beauty with wavy black hair, and eyes the color of Spode blue china.

But my dad hadn't changed much. He was still short, underweight, and needed braces for a gap in his teeth. They were almost the same age, but when he looked at her, it seemed like an impossible dream that she would keep the promise to marry him after high school. Still, he maintained that hope alive by coming over to her house as often as he could, visiting her, and helping her father with yard work and other chores as he'd always done since her father lost a hand from a work accident.

They got along well together, but she treated him as a brother, more or less, and not like he wanted her to be interested in him, like a sweetheart. And it was hard for him to see her each day as he mowed the lawn or did other things and watch other guys come over and try to spend time with her. She liked the attention but never developed any real interest in any of them. Still, when she and another boy disappeared into her room, it always made him jealous. The other boys knew he was close to her, but never considered him a threat and tried to bribe him to "get a good word in" for them.

In addition to yard work, my dad also did the cooking. My mom's mother was never much of a cook, but his mother was and taught him. That meant that he spent a lot of time in the kitchen helping make bread or fixing dinners while she was there, and they could talk. He even taught her some dishes, and that was more time together for them.

Something else that got my mom interested in him was that he developed a car salesman's persona when serving dinner. He would make outlandish statements like Tony down at the used car lot. My mom had liked the way Tony talked because he was a real character, and found Bob, my dad, just as funny and entertaining.

An example might be that he would "sell" the dishes when he put them on the table. He'd say, "This delectable pot roast has few miles on it, stops on a dime, and will give you long hours of chewing before you finally swallow it." Or, "What have we here? A chestnut brown, newly sliced loaf of bread, fresh from the oven. Won't that be a prize when you put it in your mouth!" And, "This dessert might look like Flying Possum Pie, but it's really the most delectable chocolate and pecan pie you'll ever sink your teeth into!"

His 'Flying Possum Pie' was something he'd often make as dessert. That was because my mom's dad really liked it. It was creamy, layered chocolate, and cream cheese pie in a pecan shortbread crust, which was a favorite in his family. Of course, his family didn't call it that, instead it was known merely as Chocolate Pecan Pie. The difference was that he'd bring it in and squash it down — what he called "creaming it," and then slice it for us.

Still, he was somewhat of an embarrassment to have around when guys would come over. And in their senior year, after she was made Homecoming Queen, she made excuses for why he shouldn't be there when someone would come by or take her out for a date. He could be funny in the kitchen cutting up while making dinner, that was true, but he was somewhat of a joke as anything else.

One time that really stood out was when she had several friends over —another couple and her date, and they were spending time listening to records and dancing. Dad came in and started doing tricks for them. They were card tricks mostly, and her date, the quarterback for the football team, said that that was boring. That's when my dad flopped down on his back, put his legs in the air, and lit a match. Instantly flames came out like a blowtorch towards her date. He got chased out of the house, and my mom wouldn't speak to him for weeks.

By graduation, things hadn't changed much. My mom was still a beauty, but my dad was, well, not a beauty. He went off to college in another town while she stayed local. She started attending classes at the community college while working at a pet hospital owned by an uncle. There the vet took an interest in her.

He was about ten years older than she, and had come from the nearby city, and was ex-military, having flown transports for the Air Force. He owned a small plane, a two-seat Cessna that he would operate on the weekends. He would offer to take her, but she always refused. She had gotten airsick the only time she flew, and that was in an airliner, so she knew she didn't want to go up in a small airplane. But she was thrilled when he flew because he would fly over her house and rock his wings as he passed over.

Once, when my dad was visiting, the vet came buzzing over in his plane, doing loops and dives and dipping his wings. My dad said he prayed for him to crash, especially after my mom seemed thrilled with the exhibition. But all he could do was sit and watch, as she, staring up, said things like, "Oh, isn't that marvelous!"

"Yes, it is exciting," he'd say... Thinking all the while: Hit the ground, why doncha!

It was about that time things started to change for dad. He had started running, and his lean body became toned and athletic. He'd also fixed his teeth by then and had a dazzling smile. But most of all, he became rich. Not multi-millionaire rich, but rich enough to come back home and have something to offer my mom beyond being funny and doing card tricks.

At college, he found that the food choices were few and almost inedible. So he got the idea to place a sandwich kiosk just outside the campus. He used the freshest of ingredients and gave his sandwiches crazy names, and the kiosk was an instant success. He got others involved, added morning sandwiches, and then dinner sandwiches. Finally, he offered dessert. It was a creamy, layered chocolate and pecan pie that he called... Yes, you know what it was. Flying Possum Pie.

Soon, most of the students and faculty were lined up at his places all day. The kiosk became so successful that more were placed at other spots around the campus. Then the same thing was tried at nearby colleges. In a few years, the kiosks numbered in the hundreds, and, when he got his degree in business management, he sold the booths for enough to come back home and show everyone that he did "make it big." He also married my mom.

Why? As he likes to say, it was all due to Flying Possum Pie.

MARIE BRINGS HOLLYWOOD HOME

It was a bright Summer day in August 1987, when a classmate of ours from high school, Marie Donaldson, left for Hollywood. But it was a dark day, and raining when she returned recently. She was a movie star, the first one from our town, and everyone was excited when they heard she was coming back. In her honor, several of us thought we should celebrate her return by having a parade or something. For Kanab, Utah, with a population of 3,802, it's a big deal to have a real celebrity in town.

But the day she drove into town she didn't stop under the banner that said "Welcome Back Marie" where the mayor and the band were set up to welcome her, but instead drove on to her aunt's place at the edge of town. Someone said she gave the mayor the finger, but no one else saw that. Others said she waved. No matter, the mayor gave a short speech (he was up for reelection), the band played something stirring, and the local boy scout troop started marching around while most of us left.

I mentioned that Marie was our first celebrity from Kanab, but we've had movie stars here before. The Parry Lodge on Main Street used to cater to them when film crews were in the area. Zion and Bryce Canyon National Parks are north of us and many movies have been shot near there. But that was back in the Thirties and

Forties, and those were mostly B and C westerns, with such stars as Ken Maynard, Bob Steele and Johnny Mack Brown.

For awhile, the Parry Lodge used their notoriety to draw people there. They put up the names of movies stars who stayed there above the doors of all the rooms. Of course, most of the names were unknown to most visitors, and those that were famous, such as Gene Autry and Roy Rodgers, never made a movie here. Still, it was enough for most visitors to think they were in the same room as someone they had heard of. But in order to keep things authentic, the place was never upgraded. It had been built in the early thirties and it showed: small rooms, tiny bathrooms, and no air conditioning.

So, what does the Parry Lodge have to do with Marie Donaldson? She bought the place. It had been boarded up for years, and, learning that when she returned, she bought it… Almost for the taxes still unpaid when the last owners skipped town a dozen years ago. And she did what the prior owners hadn't done; she renovated the old place, upgrading everything, included the former Western motif. You see, what Marie McDonald was known for in Hollywood were horror movies, not westerns.

She was one of the original "Scream Queens" starring in such memorable movies as "Hell House Horror," "Motel Massacre," and "Labor Day Lasher." And she seemingly kept something from those movies because when she walked around in town she was always dressed in a black dress and had on make-up that made her look like Elvira. Sure, she would say, "Hi, nice to see you," and smile, but with the way she looked, it was hard to smile back.

Also, she was different from the Marie Donaldson that most people knew from back then. She seldom looked you in the eyes, and when she did, it was a blank stare, without feelings or recognition of who you were. She'd never use your name, instead saying something general. Even her steady from high school, Don Patterson, said he couldn't get her to remember him. "She just looked straight past me," is what he said. It was eerie and disturbing, but not as much as what came next.

The old Parry Lodge had a feature visitors liked. At the edge of the parking lot was a barn that was was used for screening movies that had been filmed nearby. Every night they would set up a projector, sell popcorn and cokes, and show western movies. And on the weekends someone would come in who may have been an extra to tell about their experiences being around "real movie stars." Well, that feature was updated as well.

Marie's new look to the Parry Lodge was the spiting image of the Bates motel from Psycho. And where she got someone who looked like Norman Bates to be the clerk, was the question everyone had. Of course, she replaced the names of western stars above the doors with those who had starred in horror movies —but only those who had died in horror movies, not any of the survivors. As to the barn, that was redone to resemble the exterior of Hell House. But inside, no movies are shown. Instead a reenactment of one of her first scenes in movies, from Motel Massacre.

A troupe of young actors puts on the scene where a couple arrive on a dark and stormy night and say, 'Please, we saw the No Vacancy sign, but wouldn't you have something? We'll take anything.' The Norman Bates-look-alike smiles and says, 'Well, gee, we do have Cabin 13. Nobody likes to spend the night there, superstitions and all that. And, well, there was what happened there, what was it, thirteen years ago tonight? That's available.'

At that point the visitors are asked if they want to go to Cabin 13. Those that do tend to be disappointed. They are marched into a small space, sit on plastic folding chairs and get to watch what appears to be a reenactment of the last scene of an Ed Wood movie, Orgy of the Ghouls, that lasts all of 15 minutes that consists of hand puppets of people dying left and right, hacked to death by something lurking behind a huge black cape. Mostly it is just screams and splatters of blood. But few people stay to the end;

most leave grumbling about why in hell they came. And the die-hards who stay are left wondering why they were dumb enough not to leave.

Another tradition that began with Marie's return is that we hold a film festival in her honor once a year. For two days, we pack the Bijou theater where all of Marie's movies are shown. And that includes her first movie, Invaders From Uranus, which is always shown last but still plays to a full house. Marie is in only in one scene, where she is seen jogging and has no lines. At that point, many people stand and clap loudly. We are a close-knit com-munity and proud of it. The festival is over, really, at that point. With no more Marie in the movie and more than an hour to go, many people file out.

One thing I forgot to mention was that we learned why Marie Don-aldson had to leave Hollywood. It turns out that she was asked to do a nude scene in a movie, and she refused to do it. After that, the producer spread the word that she was "uncooperative." No one else would touch her. (Sorry about the pun.) We felt that whatever Marie was like now, whether dressing strangely or act-ing weird, it was because Hollywood made her that way. We've all seen Sunset Boulevard; we know that happens.

POEMS: THE SPHINX; THE HEART; NEVER GET MY FILL

The Sphinx

You are the Sphinx,
Sublime in the desert,
Stone-faced,
And stone-hearted;
What secrets you hold,
Have not been told,
Since Oedipus,
Had you out-smarted.

I am not Oedipus,
But a friend,
Who wants to solve
Your ancient riddle;
Let me unearth you,
From your desert sands,
Not to trick or trap you,
But meet you in the middle.

The Heart

The heart may be captured,
By word or solitary deed;
Seldom does it miss a chance,
To hopelessly concede.

Never Get My Fill

I want to see the earth from high,
while soaring, as a bird might,
above the noise, above the crowds
and without the endless plight.

Isn't the song and poetry
of the virgin earth enough?
Or must it be distorted, muted,
and hidden beneath the muck?

I wish to see the land whole,
without its many scars:
of ugly road, and ugly homes,
and lights that dim the stars.

Perhaps there still remains,
in some remote mountaintop,
A place where stars explode at night,
and nature's sounds don't stop.

I call each mountain my brother,
and give my heart to every hill.
The sweet honey of the forests,
I taste, but can never get my fill.

WHITE GOLD
TRUFFLES

Harold Jacobs was a serious man about food. He was the chef and owner of the most well-regarded and expensive restaurants in his city, Harold's Place.   Each year the owners of the city's restaurants would put on a banquet celebrating their culinary profession and award one chef with their most prestigious award, the Augie, named after the great French chef, Auguste Escoffier. Jacobs had entered the competition for 15 years straight but had never won the award. He vowed that this year, the prize would be his. His dish would be roasted lamb with white gold truffles.

For the lamb, he had enlisted the help of a farmer who found him a special breed of lamb from the isle of Gurney that was regarded as the "world's best." And the farmer would supply him with a young specimen raised on mother's milk for its first three months, and then grain-fed exclusively, resulting in virtually no "gamey" taste, but still flavorful.

For the white truffles, he would ensure they were the best. The most expensive mushrooms in the world, truffles are usually only found in a few select places in Europe. But he learned that recently they were found growing in a forest region in Wisconsin. Mushroom hunters found them at the base of several oak trees that had been dead for years, and when they reached the tables of a few select restaurants in New York, food critics them pronounced them even superior to the best from France or Italy. Their distinction was a gold hue at the top of their crowns.

Jacobs would have those for his dish. He hired those same mushroom hunters to locate more truffles for him and even sent to Europe for truffle dogs bred to sniff out truffles.

The anticipation of what Jacobs would offer as his dish at the banquet spread, and others decided that they too would look for the white truffles. In addition to the award, there was a market in white truffles, and prices ranged from $3,000 to $9,000 per pound for the delicacy. It was indeed mushroom royalty.

A week before the competition was to be held, Jacobs learned that the truffle dogs were forbidden from leaving France due to government restrictions. They were designated "national treasures" and not allowed to be exported without permits that would take months to process.

As to the two mushroom hunters, they didn't seem to fit the part when they showed up. Their names were Terrence Young and Chester Bonneville, but they went by the names Ty and Bones. Both were in their early twenties and looked more like slacker types who resembled "The Dude" from The Big Lebowski. Their bowling shirts and penchant for weed certainly didn't mark them as serious mushroom hunters. So Jacobs decided to engage a third person to join them in the hunt for the truffles, his own sous chef, Andre.

Something else worried Jacobs. Finding the truffles might not be the only difficult task. Keeping them and getting them to the restaurant might also prove increasingly difficult. Reports of others also seeking truffles either by locating them or stealing them from others were rumored. Some restaurants in New York were said to pay top prices for them, paying high prices to black-market thieves in anonymous and nefarious back-alley deals.

Thus, the journey of the three for Harold's Place was to be secretive. The three flew out to Wisconsin in a small rented plane instead of a commercial flight. They landed in a field near the place where they had found the white gold truffles previously. Andre got out with a knapsack, boots, and a flashlight and was ready. The other two said they wanted to "kick back" for a while and join Andre later. They had two-way radios and would check in within an hour. Andre smelled the weed they lit up before he got more than twenty paces away.

Truffles are typically found just beneath the surface growing on the roots of older trees, mostly oak, elm, or hazel, in soil moist from rain and beneath tree cover that shields from the most sun. And the best is on the base of dead trees that have been dead at least three years, and not more than six years. Andre scanned the surroundings as he walked into the forest.

Deep cover… Moist soil… Dead trees. That's what he looked for.

After searching for an hour, he heard the sounds of others nearby. He spoke into his radio but got no reply. Then he spotted them, a group of six or more. Were they following him? He veered off and hiked in the opposite direction at a rapid pace for two miles to lose them. He tried the radio again. Still nothing from Ty and Bones. He continued the search. It was growing dark now, but he didn't want to use his flashlight. He continued, head close to the ground, still looking for the ideal conditions —deep cover, moist soil, dead trees.

He tried the radio again. Nothing. He searched for another hour. Tried the radio again and still nothing. Feeling tired, he sat. That's when he spotted it. A small hovering craft no bigger than a dessert plate. It came up to him and stopped about a foot away. Then a voice said, "Check your radio, dummy, you have the volume turned down."

Ty and Bones told Andre that they had found white gold truffles once again soon after they employed the drone to try to make contact with him. They were in a grove of dead elms this time and were spotted from the air above the treetops. They walked straight there, dug and found three prize truffles, and were ready to leave. They would meet him on the plane.

"NO!" Andre replied. "I'm not ready to go. You might have found what you came looking for, but I haven't! Give me a couple more hours. We'll leave at midnight."

Ty and Bones agreed. But by midnight, Andre hadn't returned. They tried the radio. He didn't answer. Ty used his cell and called Jacobs. "Leave him if he doesn't show in another hour," Jacobs said. "Fly back with the truffles. That's what you were paid to do. The pilot can return for Andre in the morning."

The pilot might have done that, but in coming in for a landing, he came in too low and crashed short of the runway. There were no survivors. Jacobs rented another small plane and went himself into the forest to search for Andre. He found others there searching for the elusive white gold truffles, but not Andre. He searched for another day before giving up, called the authorities, and returned to his city.]

At the banquet, Jacob was awarded the prize he sought. He had made the dish, roasted lamb with white gold truffles, and it was the winner by a mile. But it was made with white gold truffles bought on the black market, no questions asked. His speech was memorable for what it didn't mention: the lives of his two mushroom hunters, a pilot, and probably his sous chef, Andre. He did draw out his speech and talked about the use of aviation and drones in finding the best of ingredients for dishes, but went no further. His speech was solemn and dignified, keeping with his reputation of being a serious man about food.

THE ROMANCING OF ROGER

The most beautiful girl in town was Susan Slattery. From the day she moved into Seneca Falls from nearby Syracuse when she was fourteen, no girl ever looked more attractive. She was "Hollywood beautiful." And even after she got married to Roger Greyson, had two children, and put on a few pounds, she still turned heads when she was seen in the stores or walking on Main St. And later, when she got a job at the Chandler Cafe, the older men got a chance to see her close up, and just be near someone so gorgeous.

The Chandler Cafe was the oldest diner in town, but business dropped off after another newer place, The Turnpike, located just off Highway 20, opened for business. The Turnpike had better coffee, fresh pastries baked on the premises, and twice the number of dishes on the menu. But the Chandler Cafe got all its customers back again, and more, when they hired Susan.

When Susan's shift began at seven, the Chandler was always nearly packed. She started off by taking a coffee carafe and going around the place poured them their first cup in the morning, or topping off their mugs. And she'd say, "Hi, Sweetie, coffee? How about a sweet roll to go with it? Fresh baked, just in. Or do you want some eggs this morning? Scrambled, sunny side up, or anyway you like 'em. And we got bacon, ham, and sausage to go with 'em. We can even cook you up some spinach, to stay healthy. Say, how you been? I missed you yesterday. It's good to see ya again." She warmed their hearts, and filled their stomachs.

Back in high school, she had been Miss Everything, from Homecoming Queen to lead cheerleader. Even after she started to going steady with Roger Greyston, the quarterback for the football team, she was still everyone's dream girl. She was said to be headed for Hollywood after graduation. But she got married, had a child straight away, and no one talked about her going off after that.

Susan was no bookworm, and never really had good grades, but she started taking classes at the community college after her first born was six months old. But then she got pregnant again and never finished her degree program. A job as a receptionist at the insurance company in town was her first job, but she didn't last more than a few weeks. She had to type, but had never learned how, and that cost her her job. The waitressing job was a good fit. Since Roger could only find part time work, he could see to the kids in the morning. And when she returned home in the afternoon, he went off to his job, and worked late most nights.

The men at Chandlers always asked about her husband.

"So," they'd say, "how's Roger?"

"All right, I suppose."

"Don't you see him?"

"Not much lately."

"Hmmm. You still married, aren't you?"

"Of course... Happily."

"Happily?"

"As happily as possible, given things."

"Like what kinda things?"

Susan would usually change the subject then, or laugh, or say something like "Life things, you know." It was hard for Susan to talk it, but she was not happy with her marriage. She still loved Roger, but it wasn't the dream life that she thought she'd have with him. And it wasn't the fault of Roger. He was good to her, took care of the kids better than most dads, but he didn't provide much of anything else otherwise. He worked down at a quarry almost two hours away, and even though he put in few hours there, with the commute, he arrived back home close to midnight when she was asleep. And she was up at six so she could get to Chandler's by seven.

For the most part, Susan's romance came from books. Her Aunt Millicent gave Susan her first romance paperback written by Romana Robinson, the romance queen of Swashbuckling pirate epics, and after that Susan became addicted. She could escape her almost romance-free existence by going to sea with pirates, sea captains or governor's aides, engulfed in a tide of liquid prose about fetching damsels and things they did that made her blush when she read them.

She'd go beyond the cover —always featuring the most strikingly handsome, chiseled faces, and bare chests, muscled and toned, and her simple apartment became a colonial plantation located in the Caribbean, on the island of Nevis or Hispaniola. Suave nobleman or robust scalawags would find their way to her looking to ravish her or worse. And then leave her in disgrace, in tattered remnants of her slinky silk or gossamers-thin nightgown and a dim recollection of an episode of abandon.

"I never thought I'd like them as much as I do," she told her aunt, "but now that I do, I hate myself for escaping this way."

"Probably half the women of America read them," her aunt said. "Over 5,000 new ones come out each year. That's each year! You just got started early, that's all. Your Roger turned into his dad far too quickly."

"So, how do I get Roger back to being the Roger I married?"

"You've been married now —is it fourteen years? He's not going back to what he was like back then. That guy is gone."

Susan looked astonished, then quizzical. "Really?"

Millicent sighed and then took Susan's face in her hands. "You wait for him to come back and you'll wait forever. You have to make him the best new version of Roger. That's who you have to find."

Susan's face brightened as if a light had gone on inside her. She nodded her head, several times, as new revelations occurred to her.

"And honey," her aunt said, "you have to do something with yourself first. You could do so much with what you have, which is quite a lot. You put on too much weight with the babies. Maybe thirty pounds —am I right?"

Susan put her head down, patted down her skirt, and said, "More like forty."

Millicent took Susan's hand, "Most of that has to go. You're only five foot two. you can't carry all that weight. And then see Margie over at the Best Beauty Salon to give you a new style and color. She can make anyone a bombshell… Mommy or not. See me after that. I have some nighties I haven't worn since I lost my Clarence, They'll fit you. Or we could go to Syracuse and get you some new things."

When she got home, Susan felt bad. She knew she had been neglecting herself and Dennis. And she would work her tail off to change things. First, she would lay off the doughnuts in the morning, scones in mid afternoon, and eat healthy otherwise. No second helpings, and no snacks while reading her books. Of course, it was tough cutting back on sweets when she was saying to customers, "Have a slice of pie for dessert? The Banana Cream really looks special today. Care for some cake? Chocolate lava, caramel custard, and New York style cheesecake are all on display. Or, what about ice cream? We got ten flavors, and lots of toppings for ya."

But Susan was determined. Within the first week, she had dropped five pounds. The next week the loss was only two pounds, but she kept at it. By the end of the third week she had picked up a pound, which surprised her. But she stuck to her plan: no sweets. And to try to take off weight, she decided to do exercises. After the kids were asleep, she went down into the basement did cheerleading routines there. They were hard to do at first, but she stuck with it. She did ten minutes of cheerleading the first night, then fifteen minutes, and she was up to thirty minutes by weeks end.

While doing the cheerleading exercises, Susan thought about why she was doing it. Was it to get a new Roger? Or maybe it was to get a new Susan instead? Did she really want that? Other people had said the same thing that her aunt said, the changes she needed to make, and she'd thought about it herself. But everything she thought of doing, she knows of others, many of them, who did make themselves over and didn't really like themselves after that. And their husbands didn't either.

One person, Denise, ended up going to California to start a new life there. Was that where this would end? And she heard of others, from high school, who changed things too much. And they weren't happy after all. They found other guys, but creepy guys, not so nice, and that was bad. And Pam, someone who changed the most, got so stuck-up that nobody wanted to be with her.

Susan stopped her her cheerleading routines. She also stopped sipping sweets, and stopped making plans to change herself. She went back to her romance novels, back to eating sweets, and back to being the best waitress, mother and wife she could be. Better to be what feels right. No sense in changing things unless they're broke. And right now, romance can be enjoyed, and left behind, in books that aren't really real, but what can be dreamed about, while living in the real world.

POEMS: DADDY'S DREAM; NATURE'S KIN; A DEMON

Daddy's Dream

My Daddy aimed for bigger things
Than just owner of a grocery,
But Mama, his newly wedded wife,
Said, "Abe, now we are a family."

It wasn't that he couldn't achieve,
His goal of going into law,
It was because Mama said,
"We've got a child, and now you are a Pa."

So he put his plans on hold
While he worked to keep us fed,
And while he built a life for us,
He killed his dream instead.

He rose each day at half past six,
To get to the produce mart by nine;
And make it back, ate a snack,
Opening the grocery doors on time.

They bought a house right behind,
A tract home that wasn't much to see.
But they filled it to the brim with love,
For one another first, then for their only child, me.

Mama found him at his desk one day
Tears filled his aging eyes.
He was looking at his high school pics,
There was sadness she could spy.

"Abe," she said, "What's on your mind,
I see your restlessness."
"You know I'm not the wandering kind,"
He said, "But I must confess."

The fire in his eyes shone bright,
And his words didn't seem so sad.
"This is not the life I wanted,
Yet I couldn't be more glad."

"You are the dearest wife to me,
But I'm restless, that is true.
I am not what I thought I'd be,
But being a grocer meant that I had you."

I wrote this poem because I know,
That what I have achieved,
Is only due, to what my dad did too,
And what I am is what he bequeathed.

Nature's Kin

Daughter of the sun,
Child of the Moon,
You are nature's kin.
Take your breath
Along a mountain crest,
And your wild heart does sing.

You are a pinecone
Covered with dew;
You are spring flowers,
With kaleidoscope hue;
You are the wind,
That rustles the leaves;
You are the sum
Of all that you see.

Daughter of the sun,
Child of the moon,
With all nature you agree;
You were born,
Under Capricorn,
To live among your family.

A Demon

I am a demon
from the darkest nightmare,
formed in the fires
of the foulest hell.

I came to impart
more fear and despair
to wretched lives
where nothing is well.

I found you alone,
Venus on her shell,
ready and waiting,
a babe ready to snatch.

You were so calm
with no fear of hell
that it made me wonder
if I'd met my match.

You welcomed me in,
open arms and wide legs,
and made my desires
awake in such haste.

You were done in a flash
and left me with dregs
leaving me famished
after only a taste.

What were the lessons
you taught me that night?
And what can a demon
gain from such fright?

Whatever they were
you did not disclose;
for demons and devils
should never repose.

I'LL BE HOME FOR CHRISTMAS

Doris left her apartment late morning, well after she had intended to. Would she get to her parent's house before nightfall? She would if she didn't stop for lunch and just got drive-through and ate along the way. Was there something fresh and healthy along the Turnpike? No McDonald's certainly, and no hamburger place of any sort. No, it had to really wholesome and organic, if possible. If only there were a place like Mendocino Farms, her favorite for sandwiches, or even Subway, somewhere around Franklin or Pottsville. She should have checked the internet, but there wasn't time.

She decided to go to her parents for Christmas just that morning, after that fight with Jeff. She'll show him. Arguing with her over such a minor thing... Really?

Packing was a nightmare. Did she want to spend just a couple of nights over the extended weekend? Or the entire week that she got off of work? She compromised —what Jeff should have done— and packed for five days.

She hadn't been to her parent's place since last Summer. And not for Christmas at their place since... When was that? Was it five years ago now? She always promised she'd make it, but things always came up at the last minute.

Was the radio always this bad? She couldn't get a decent station. No easy listening on FM. And those horrible talk shows talking nonsense about things they know nothing about. And sports talk… How can they fill air time with that? And preachers, the worse. How can you hear the word of God barreling along the highway at seventy-five mph?

In the back seat were presents she got at the last minute. Gift baskets from the supermarket: One that that tins of different teas from around the world. Another that had beers from around the world. And the third a variety of Jerky, also from around the world. Funny, they looked similar. Better make sure I get the right ones for the right people, she thought. My parents get the teas, Jerky for Gordon, and the beers for Larry. Gordon and Larry won't be there, but just in case they are….

Also in the backseat was file work that she wanted to get done while at her parents. Doris was a paralegal at a law firm. She had about ten hours of work that she brought with her. And if things got too dull for her, she could do some work on a project that would amount to another ten hours. Her last visit to her parents on Christmas was quiet, too quiet, and at least this time it could be productive.

There it was, Highway 26, the turnoff… Only about twenty miles to their place. What should she tell them about what was going on in her life? Basically, all they wanted to know if she was engaged now, and when the wedding was. Her job? Her career? Or how she was doing in her college classes? Those things never interested her parents. But they were priorities to her. Marriage? She had been married before and wanted to get it right this time.

She pulled up the driveway and parked by the back wall. She got out the gift baskets and office work. The suitcases would be left for later. She walked up the three steps to the backdoor and put her hand on the cold brass knob. It felt freezing and chilled her in a way she couldn't remember experiencing before. She shuddered slightly and then went in. "Hello," she said as she walked into the mudroom, closed the door, and began to take off her coat.

"Damn!" She said, out loud. "Are you trying to save money or what?" It was colder inside than it was outside.

"Mom, Dad, I'm home."

Nothing was heard. And no lights were on even though it was getting dark.

Louder this time, "MOM! DAD! I'M HOME!"

Still, nothing was heard. She walked into the hallway and then into the living room. The Christmas tree was up in the same place, near the piano, but unlit. And she noticed that the fish tank was also unlit and empty of fish. Did Mom's orange and silver guppies all die? She put the gifts under the tree... The only ones there. Well, maybe they're out buying things at the last minute, she thought. That's unlike them.

She walked into her room and put her office work down on the dresser. She looked into the mirror. *Shame on you for not calling and letting them know you're coming,* she scolder herself. They might be out having dinner somewhere or visiting someone. Do I call them now? No use. They don't have cellphones. I'd be calling the house. She sat on the bed. What to do? She got out the office work and started sorting through it. Then she thought, something's wrong.

Doris recalled always hearing music in the house at Christmastime. Always. Her mother loved the Time-Life Treasury of Christmas albums and seemed to play them continuously from Thanksgiving until Christmas Day. And she would have candles and the smell incense in the house. Not today. Something was definitely wrong.

Then she heard a door creak open. Finally, they're home.

Wait! That's the front door that creeks that way, not the back door.

She waited. Silence. Then the sound of someone slowly walking in the house in their boots. Mom and Dad wouldn't do that. They'd take them off in the mudroom.

The footsteps went into the kitchen and then came back toward the bedrooms. Doris held her breath.

A silhouette pushed the door open. "Hey, Freckles," said the figure, "how come you're hiding out in your room?" It was her brother, Larry. "And where is everyone?"

Doris breathed finally. Color returned to her face as she said, "That's what I've been trying to figure out. I just got here myself about half an hour ago. And nobody was home."

"Yeah, and nothing in the kitchen to eat. That's strange. I figured dinner about six, and it's almost that now."

"They're probably having dinner out, after doing last-minute shopping," said Doris.

"Last minute shopping and dinner out? Mom and Dad? Mom thinks it's a sin not to have her Christmas shopping done by Labor Day. And Dad thinks it's a mortal sin to eat out *ever*."

Doris smiled. "Maybe they've changed."

"They're Lutheran fundamentalists. They get more set in their ways, not less."

Doris laughed. "Original sin is a powerful thing to atone for, but they keep trying."

And you forget being worthless and vile unless you feel guilty for it."

"How can I forget if they keep mentioning it?" Said Doris.

They both laughed. And then stopped. The back door slammed hard.

"Gordon!" They both said almost in unison.

Yes, it was The Golden Boy, as he was known to the financial world of commodities and trade futures, come home. But to Doris and Larry, it was just Gordon… And sometimes Goliath because he was so big and hulking and did everything with a lot of noise.

"Did hell freeze over this year?" Larry said when Gordon popped his head into Doris's room.

"No, just like salmon going back to where they were spawned, I was drawn back by forces bigger than myself."

"Something bigger than you?" Said Doris, with a smile. "That's hard to believe."

Gordon looked to the ceiling, and possibly the heavens beyond, "I don't understand it myself. I wasn't expecting to come because I couldn't come. It was out of the question again this year, but here I am. Christmas exerts powerful forces."

"You're all alone this year, is that it?" Doris said.

Gordon chuckled. "Right. I'm in-between fashion models."

"And what's your story, Miss Omaha Law?" Said Gordon.

"I fought with Jeff. Nothing that won't sort itself out after Christmas… Probably in time for New Year's."

"And you, Mr. Property Manager, what's your story?" Gordon said to Larry.

"Like you, I turned a corner in one of my mall properties, and some bars of a Christmas tune I hadn't heard in years came on. Something clicked inside my head. Then, like the waters of the great Mississippi River flowing into the Gulf of Mexico, I cascaded here.

"In other words, you're also alone this Christmas." Said Gordon with a smirk.

"Exactly."

"So," said Gordon, "where are they?"

They found the note their parents left on the refrigerator door. It read this way:

Doris, Gordon, and Larry.

We don't know if you will come home for Christmas. We've extended invitations to all three of you for the last five years, but you haven't made it back. This year we decided to visit Aunt Margie. As you know, her Harold passed away a few weeks ago, and this will be her first Christmas without him. That's where we are. If you do come home and don't want to be by yourself, go over to the Reverend Johansson and his wife. That's where we would be if we were home.

Merry Christmas!

The Reverend Johansson and his wife were in the middle of dinner when they heard the knock on the door. They had been arguing whether or not to make such a big dinner, year after year, when people that say they will come, don't show up, and how wrong it is to do that. "Hello," said Doris, "Merry Christmas." She had a gift basket of tins of teas from around the world in her hands.

"Merry Christmas," said Gordon, who was right behind Doris. He had a gift basket of beef jerky from around the world.

Larry was behind Gordon. "Reverend, how are you? Merry Christmas! Aren't you going to invite us in?" Under his arm was a gift basket featuring beers from around the world.

The Reverend said, "Come right in! Merry Christmas to you all!" He was happy because he had won the bet with his wife. If no one showed this Christmas, he would wash, dry and put away all the dishes. He couldn't help but say to his wife as he walked back into the dining room, "Look who has dropped by for Christmas dinner. This is what Christian charity is all about!"

HENRIETTA REVISED ON ROMANCE

Henrietta Hollingsworth disliked romance novels. No, she hated them intensely and always had since she first saw a few in the supermarket's paperback section. That they multiplied almost like rabbits and took over most of the paperback section only infuriated her more. However, she liked to read Jane Austen, and she considered it a truth, universally acknowledged, that Austen was not a romance novel author.

Austen's books were beautifully written, Henrietta thought, with authentically detailed settings, realistic dialogue, and amusing subplots. They had psychological depth to them, finely crafted characters and universal themes of societal morals, manners, traditions, duty to society, and religious seriousness. She remembered reading something similar to that on the back of one of Austen's books.

Romance novels were just lurid covers and improbable fantasies. She read that somewhere as well.

One day Henrietta noticed that a few romance novels were placed at the check-out stands. Horrors! Then, more of them appeared there. Still more the next time she was at the supermarket. She commented to the cashier, "Why bring all those disgusting books up here? What was management thinking? I wouldn't read that trash if I were on a desert island, and it was the only thing available."

The cashier looked at Henrietta for a moment and deigned to make any reply, but finally said, "Have you read any?"

"Absolutely not!" Henrietta said, indignantly.

"How about I let you borrow one of mine? I just finished it." The cashier said. Then she reached under the counter, took out her purse, pulled a book from it, and put it into the bag she was filling with Henrietta's groceries. The cover had a bosomy dark-haired temptress in a pink gown being held, arms back, by a blond-haired Viking, bare-chested, but wearing a horned helmet, with one of the horns almost touching her jutting, quivering breasts. "Read a few pages, and then tell me what you think."

"Get that disgusting thing out of my groceries!" Henrietta said.

The cashier looked around to see if anyone else heard. No one did. Still concerned, she said, "The groceries are on me. Just read a few pages."

Henrietta thought a moment, then nodded her head, okay. She left with a smile on her face. Once outside, she took the book out of the grocery bag to throw it away. At the trash can, she stopped. It would only be fair to read some of it, given that she got free groceries.

She started reading, and suddenly her legs became wobbly, her face turned crimson, and she was only on page 9. By page 27, as she sat on the window ledge, her frozen peas were thawing, and her ice cream was melting. She needed to get home.

No, first she needed to find out if Margo would ever escape from Erik, and what was that he did to her that made her such a slave to him in his bed chambers. And maybe more about milky white skin pressed against scars, tight pert body parts being stretched beyond limits, and, Good Lord, more mentions of the most unmentionable things possible!

Just then, a shadow fell on her book. Henrietta looked up, and there's the cashier standing with a knowing grin. "Want me to put your frozen things back in the freezer?" She said.

POEMS: THE LIGHTEST THING; A FLOWER; THE MOVIES

The Lightest Thing

I am but the lightest thing
Underneath the summer sun.
I will fly on feathered wing
Until the day is done.

I will soar by cliffs and clouds
And like a dancer twirl the ground.
Watch me spin and watch me stop
On the highest hill around.

When the light begins to fade
And I must come down again
I'll thank the birds that set me free
And the golden day my friend.

A Flower

I held a flower in my hands,
On a day quite warm and fair,
And then nodded off to sleep,
And dream, but was unaware,
That the flower grew quite tall
And danced, a gentle petal dance.
Be aware: flowers can be more,
Than what they seem at first glance

The Movies

From the tongue of Tom Hanks
I learned the common lessons of life;
And Meryl Streep made me yearn
For the love and sweetness of a wife.

Movie houses were my temples
Where I learned to cry and crave;
Fantasies that always promised,
But seldom ever gave.

Life and romance is not that simple:
Easy answers and easy bliss;
When the actors went home at night
It was not to a life like this.

THE PRICE AND PRIVILEGE OF HOMICIDE.

few years ago, when Donald Trump was a candidate for the presidency, he declared, "I could stand in the middle of Fifth Avenue and shoot somebody, and I wouldn't lose any voters." Of course, he was being a blowhard and bragging about the loyalty of his followers. But when I read that statement, it took me back almost fifteen years to when I heard something almost identical said by another billionaire who did mean it because he had gotten away with murder.

It was the summer of 2005, and the notion of a rich man openly bragging that he could get away with murder didn't seem too unusual given the setting and circumstance. It was at a pool party in Pasadena among the "old money" set, and late at night when inhibitions are often set aside, and the truth filters out after too many drinks. The murder happened three decades before, and the person who said that seemed confident enough he would never incur the consequences to give details about it and the names of the people involved.

Later, I entered the names the billionaire mentioned in my computer and learned enough to suspect he might have been right. And after doing an extensive investigation that lasted several months, I concluded that the billionaire, the heir to one of America's great fortunes, had committed murder, taking a knife from his kitchen and turned it into a murder weapon—then conspiring with the local authorities to cover it up.

It happened on Saturday, October 8, 1976, according to a news account in the Los Angeles Times. The lead story read this way:

"Pasadena police this morning investigated the death of a gardener, Carlos Hernandez, who was stabbed to death by his employer, Benjamin Harding Reynolds, after mistaking him for a burglar. Mr. Reynolds, a long time resident of Pasadena, and principal owner of Reynolds Enterprises, was questioned but not detained. Police refused to indicate if Reynolds would be questioned again or be charged with criminal liability. The only witness to the stabbing was a housekeeper, Becky Gomez, who was questioned and later admitted to Huntington Memorial Hospital suffering from severe shock."

Was the death of Carlos Hernandez the result of a mistake? Or did a billionaire use his money and influence to escape criminal liability? The more I dug into the mystery, the more I saw it as a story about class, privilege, and the concentration of wealth, which resonates more than ever in the Trump era.

Of course I know that in revealing all that I learned I run the risk of losing everything that I have achieved and acquired in my life, including my reputation. I know that I might be risking my life, as others have "disappeared" for far less. Nevertheless, I will take that risk. That's how much I believe this is the right thing to do.

*****

When I started my research, I was surprised by the number of Pasadena residents with passionate opinions about the "stabbing," even after many years. On one popular Pasadena Facebook group, members regularly dissected the details of the case. Using that portal as a starting point, I reached out to people who claimed to have personal knowledge of the stabbing or its aftermath. One was Claire Evans, whose late mother, Priscilla, was the Police Chief's secretary at the time and was privy to much of what the police gathered in the way of information.

Claire is adamant about what she said: "My mother always said Reynolds bought the city of Pasadena and got away with murder. She read the full police report and knew that there was a cover-up. After she retired and we drove past the new police station, all state of the art, she'd say, 'Blood money paid for all this.' "

Denise Curran's Facebook entries stood out too. Her father had been a security guard at the Reynold mansion on what Denise called "that horrible night." She posted this conservation with her father: "The help were all in shock. When I came into the kitchen, they were crying and holding each other. I believe they all thought it was no accident. And after speaking to them, I felt the same way."

Still another person with some knowledge was Kevin Stallman. He was a rookie patrolman who was first on the scene because he was nearby when it happened and was there within minutes of the first call to police. He'd just gone on duty when the radio in his patrol unit crackled with word of an accident. He hit the roof lights and sped to the mansion.

This is from his report: "There was a blood trail from the garden to the house and women inside screaming in Spanish," he says in his account. "I didn't understand what they were saying, but they were distraught. I followed the blood trail through several rooms and found someone underneath a table, all rolled up. I was inexperienced and young, so I blurted out, 'I found him. He's under the dining room table.' That sent the housekeeper into hysterics. She jumped about frantically, and I had to subdue her. And in holding her down, she collapsed and went into shock. Thank God, there was a young nurse who happened to be walking by outside who heard the screams and came into the house to offer help. Her name was Miriam Wiggins, and I asked if she could first check the person under the table to see if he was still alive. I was focused on the housekeeper whom I held in my arms."

A short time later, a detective arrived, Joseph Tillman, and he took charge. However, his investigation was never made public.

I also identified at least a dozen other individuals who had some contact with the case, but none were as crucial as those I mentioned. That is, other than that of Benjamin Harding Reynolds.

Of course, there are photos of the scene, diagrams, an autopsy, and numerous other items taken from the scene, including the knife. Oh, the knife. I spent an entire week on that alone.

Why is all this important to me? Besides being a good citizen? I am related to someone who worked for the Pasadena Police Department, an uncle, Jack Villanueva, who was on the force. My uncle had the reputation of being a straight arrow. He wasn't allowed even to see the file, let alone take part in the investigation. Now I understand why.

But did I take this too far? My girlfriend thought so, and now she's gone. Yes, I do become obsessed sometimes. And once I get on something like this, I don't give it up until it's completed. I thought a great wrong had been done, and some sense of justice needed to meted out. Why? Because virtually everything that I learned about the case seemed to indicate that all the officials involved were paid off, threatened, or a combination of both. And that wasn't right.

For example, on October 12, 1976, the Pasadena Daily News reported this: "The Pasadena police announced today that Dr. Philip C. Ferguson, acting state medical examiner, said Carlos Hernandez died instantly of trauma to the heart after being stabbed once by a person or persons unknown."

The story didn't reveal that Dr. Ferguson weeks after that statement announced his retirement to go into private practice. And he became the personal physician to Reynolds, at a salary that was triple what he had been making as the acting state medical examiner. He also moved to the Dominican Republic and occupied a mansion there on the beach near the resort of Punta Cana. That made it impossible for state investigators to question him. In effect, the man legally charged with determining the official cause of death had gone on the payroll of the man who killed him.

But before Ferguson left the States, and while acting as the personal physician of Reynolds, he had advised police investigators that Reynolds was emotionally unable to give additional details beyond the first account. "It would have been inhumane to make him recall the tragedy again so often," he told the reporter for the Pasadena Daily News.

*****

On the last day of his life, Carlos Hernandez got up early. He'd spent a restless night tossing and turning, waking up numerous times until he finally uttered the words "Fuck it!" — threw off the covers and stomped off to the bathroom, kicking at a footstool as he passed it. His quarters were above the garage and were quite large and grand by most standards. That he occupied a two thousand square foot apartment on the grounds of the 12-acre estate was unusual. None of the other servants who worked at the Reynolds mansion lived on-site, not the butler, cook or two maids, nor the four security staff. The butler and the others loyally cared for Reynolds, but there was disapproval of his homosexuality. Most of them were from Mexico originally, where that was still considered a sin.

Although Carlos's job title was gardener, two gardeners came onto the property during the day to do the actual gardening work. As most who worked for Reynolds knew, Carlos's real job was to be an intimate companion to Reynolds. Before Carlos coming on the scene, the same apartment was occupied by a personal trainer. Before that to an interior decorator, all of whom were of Latin descent, young, and strikingly handsome. Reynolds was not openly gay, but outside the mansion, his lifestyle gave little indication of that.

Reynolds had been married twice. The first lasted less than a year. The second lasted less than six months before the couple officially separated, but no divorce ever occurred. It may have been a "marriage of convenience" because his wife took possession of an estate in Hawaii purchased before the wedding, deeded to her, and a sizable yearly allowance in the millions to maintain a grand lifestyle. And the two men who preceded Hernandez also received houses and sizable benefits when they were displaced. But the situation with Hernandez was different. Unlike the others, it was Hernandez who wanted to end the relationship with Reynolds. But nobody left Reynolds without consequences.
And the day when Hernandez was going to let him know that was the day he died.

The handsome Hernandez, a decorated hero from the Korean War, was somewhat of a Renaissance man, having apprenticed in his native Spain as a landscape artist and done work as a concept artist for the film industry in Spain, before immigrating to the States and working in Hollywood before going the Army with his lover in an odd show of Machismo. He was also a writer of poetry, a musician and singer, and a sculptor. An amateur Botanist, having learned from his father who taught Botany in Spain, he also did landscape designs. He had used many of those talents on the Frank Sinatra, Cary Grant, Sophia Loren film, The Pride and the Passion, where he was credited with working with the production designer and the art director. It was there on location in Spain for the movie that Reynolds met Hernandez.

Reynold had many relationships during his lifetime, but none as long as the one with Hernandez, which lasted more than ten years. In contrast, both of the two men who had preceded him in the apartment over the garage lived there less than a year. Most lasted a few days, if not just one night. Notoriously jealous and known for his violent temper, he'd once stabbed his first wife's in-law after they exchanged heated words. And there were other displays of anger toward others, included one that involved scissors that sent someone for attention at the ER and required twenty stitches for a wound. And Hernandez had been warned by others that Reynolds might overreact to his pending departure.

Late on the night before the stabbing, Hernandez and Reynolds had a heated argument, overheard by the estate's staff. Later, when they went out to dinner, the pair seemed to be on good terms. The staff had left by the time the couple returned to the mansion.

According to Reynolds, he stabbed someone he thought was an intruder in the dining room, which surprised him in the early morning's semi-darkness. That was the substance of his statement. But there was no further questioning about why Reynolds was holding a kitchen knife, how Hernandez got in since security staff was on duty at the time and no alarm from the very sophisticated security system sounded, and why there was a blood trail from the garden into the house that led to where Hernandez lay. Also, Hernandez's body had multiple wounds, several of them were life-ending, in addition to the one that punctured his heart.

Despite massive injuries to his lungs, heart, kidneys, and other internal organs, Hernandez did not die instantly. He may have lain there for over an hour before 911 was called. Ninety-six hours later, with no inquest—and basing their account of the incident entirely on Reynolds' word, Pasadena police chief Joseph A. Nabors declared the death accidental.

At odds with what Reynolds had said, the stabbing occurred at approximately seven-thirty, and the sun rose that day at 6:42 AM. And the fatal wound was to the heart, apparently sustained while

Hernandez was under the dining room table. Reynold would have to have crouched and gone under the table to stab him there. This was documented by the first officer on the scene who also pulled out a pad to sketch the scene. "I walked into the dining room following the blood trail, and, looked down under the large dining table, I saw a pool of blood surrounding a body that was pulled together in a fetal position," he says. "I drew a diagram of what I thought had been the point of impact between Reynolds and the body on the floor—and I could not believe what Reynolds said." In the drawing, the fatal impact—based on the blood and human remains he'd found—occurred not in the dining room but out in the garden.

Unclear as to who Hernandez was—or his relation to the man he now realized was Reynolds—the officers' first thought was that there were multiple stabbings of the body at numerous places, beginning in the garden, at several points leading to the dining room. Then several more times while the man was under the table. "I submitted my findings," he recounts, "and the next day, I got called in by my sergeant. He took me back up to the scene and showed me markings he said were inconsistent with what I had described. It became apparent things had been changed by someone so that my original sketch was rendered inconsistent I was told to change it, but I refused to do that."

According to Sergeant Norris, Officer Stallman's sketch was incorrect because it was done in the heat of the moment while he was tending to a hysterical person. "That was why it was at odds with the statements of the first detective on the case," he says. "Then, at some point, after the captain of the watch arrived, a new set of sketches were done, and they were consistent with pictures taken. The fatal stabbing happened in the dining room, the intruder crawled under the table and died there. As to the so-called "blood trail," some traces of blood were found elsewhere, but they were likely the result of people stepping into the blood in the dining room and leaving traces of it elsewhere. That would account for why anyone thought the additional stabbings occurred elsewhere."

Yet, if Reynolds said what was correct, that would still not explain what he was doing with a kitchen knife, nor what he was doing there when he usually got up after ten in the morning.

What happened later to Stallman was probably the result of his refusal to change his report. Accused of theft from the evidence room, he was given a choice to be brought up on charges, have his employment terminated, face possible criminal prosecution; or resign. He chose the latter. I tried to contact Stallman, but his whereabouts were unknown. He left the state shortly after he resigned, and no further information on him was available. I even sent Stallman's report to the best investigator I know, someone who never fails to find someone if they exist, but he was unable to locate him. It was as if he had "vanished into thin air," as the saying goes.

The first time the Pasadena PD was able to sit with and thoroughly question Reynolds was on Sunday, October 9, two days after the incident. It was a brief interview conducted in his mansion and in the presence of three attorneys for Reynolds. One was a criminal defense attorney; another was a civil attorney and the third his Chief Counsel at Reynolds Enterprises. Reynolds also had his business manager there, his Director of Personal Relations, and his business manager. Lieutenant Frank Walsh took her statement along with Detective George Watts.

Reynold gave a statement, but only limited questions were allowed to be asked. That was on his doctor's warning that Reynolds was taking medication that might hamper his ability to testify, and any stress put on him might be emotionally detrimental. A bedside encounter produced the first of two "official statements" by Reynolds. Both were contained in the formal police report, which had gone missing for decades. That is, until I began my investigation, when a government official heard that I was digging into the Hernandez killing matter and thought the truth should come out. Within a few days, the long-lost 16-page file was emailed to me.

The report, which I have since authenticated, contained two "interviews" with Reynolds. The first, dated October 9, was a brief, four-question transcript of the dining room statement. The next day the Chief of Police summarized that account for the Associated Press, adding that "It was clear that an accident occurred. Reynolds was defending himself from what he thought was a burglar. Hernandez was wounded and fell, later dying before police arrived minutes later." Calling the incident "an unfortunate accident," he said the police would take no further action. Case closed.

But almost immediately, Nabors was criticized by the state's attorney general, J. Joseph Nugent, who announced that he was "dissatisfied" with the weekend investigation. The chief also came under fire for releasing scant information to the press, as reflected in a front-page story in the Los Angeles Times, headlined: "COPS CLAM UP ON REYNOLDS KILLING." So Nabors quickly walked back his verdict, insisting that the probe was still open. Yet nothing further was done on the case, effectively closing it.

Although the police did nothing further, Reynolds or others acting on his behalf did.

Just eight days later, Reynolds donated $75,000 (equal to $500,000 today) to restore the historical library, built during the 1890s in Art Nouveau style. He also gave more than $100,000 to Pasadena Hospital, where he'd been sequestered on the night Hernandez was killed. In the following months, he began to set up the Pasadena Restoration Foundation, which, in time, would renovate over a hundred buildings from the 1880's era and the founding of the city. And that's not all. Seven months after Hernandez's death, Nabors retired, eventually purchasing a pair of Florida condos. The inspector who had questioned Reynolds after the incident was named Nabors's replacement, leapfrogging over his logical successor, the detectives' captain, to become the new chief. Another cop who had interviewed Reynolds was promoted to sergeant.

Many were surprised by Reynold's sudden burst of philanthropy. Previous to that, Reynolds had never taken an interest in the city, and had never contributed anything to its preservation. Hernandez's niece, his only heir, saw it as a cover-up. Elena Hernandez was his brother's daughter, age 19 at the time of Hernandez's death, and had been receiving money from him for college expenses. What's more, Reynolds refused to continue the payments and went on to wage a protracted court battle, refusing to settle with her and two other heirs, who had been willing to accept as little as $50,000 in damages—at a time when Reynolds was making $1 million a week in interest alone on his investments, in addition to his earnings from Reynolds Enterprises. The parties later settled for $5,000 each.

Mysteriously, the entire case file for the wrongful-death lawsuit has vanished from the Pasadena Courthouse Archives. Similarly, the record of the police investigation of the case was reported missing from the Pasadena Police Department. Even the negatives of the photographs taken that day at the mansion, which made the front page of the Pasadena Daily News the next day, disappeared from the archives at the newspaper.

So what actually happened on the day that Hernandez died? Only one person knew for sure, and that was Reynolds. He admitted to stabbing Hernandez, but his excuse that he didn't know it was Hernandez doesn't hold up for many reasons. There have been various theories about the circumstances and the actual reasons why Reynolds stabbed Hernandez and what they were doing out there in the garden before that.

One possible reason they were out there at that time in the morning seems plausible is something that Linda Gomez, the chauffeur's daughter, said. She insists, "My mom told me that they were there because of some spiritual thing; they were into new age stuff and did things like that at sunrise." This fits into accounts from others that Reynolds and Hernandez would sometimes drive out to a spiritual retreat in the Malibu canyon area to watch the sunrise.

"He had an MG sports car," said a friend of Hernandez, Paulo Arnez, "and once a month or so they'd hop over to an old boy scout camp near Malibu and mix it up with celebs like Natalie Wood and Robert Wagner, smoke pot, drink wine, sing, and dance, sometimes without clothes, and just do their thing. And sometimes they'd skip the long drive and just do their thing there at the mansion."

But what caused Reynolds to stab Hernandez? An explanation for this might have to do with something said by Vic Tanny, a neighbor of Reynolds. Before the stabbing, Tanny, like many locals, had had his own run-ins with Reynolds. For years, Tanny had an issue with trees on the Reynolds grounds that had grown so large that they were causing problems, breaking up the cement wall that separated their properties and allowing the unleashed German shepherds that served as security dogs for Reynolds to roam the Tanny grounds as well, causing multiple attacks on guests of his, as well as passerby since Tanny's estate was not fully enclosed. In May 1969, after two guests of Tanny were victimized in a single week. Tanny got a court order calling for the "removal or destruction" of the two dogs. Reynold retaliated by coming onto his property and threatening Tanny with a large bowie knife. "I've cut people with this," Reynolds said, and seemingly meant it. Later, a lawsuit filed by a delivery man claimed Reynolds stabbed him with the Bowie knife. As part of the settlement, and on direction by his lawyers, Reynolds got rid of the knife.

Thus, when provoked, Reynolds might be capable of using a knife. What may have triggered Reynold to use the knife on Hernandez remains a mystery. But a precursor to this might be what happened to a beautiful young woman named Ellen Reynolds, who became enchanted with Cisneros, the love interest of Reynolds before Hernandez. She disappeared without a trace (once again) after she was spotted dancing with him "too tightly," according to Reynolds. That angered him, and she was gone.

Thus, virtually everything that may have happened on the day Hernandez was stabbed had happened before, as if it was a "script" meant to be played out again. Was I right in all this? I still questioned myself because I was not an expert on criminal investigations. So I sought out someone who was.

"Very little about how the Pasadena police handled this had anything to do with a responsible homicide investigation," said retired LAPD detective James Radick, who has cleared hundreds of murder cases for Rampart Homicide. In 2018, I asked him to visit me to examine the evidence I'd uncovered. "You'd absolutely want to question witnesses in-depth on the relationship between the killer and decedent to determine if the death involved 'intent.' But they wrapped this one up based on a fabricated Q&A requested by the person-of-interest's own lawyers. Astonishing."

I submitted all of the evidence I accumulated to Thomas Nagasaki, a consulting pathologist and former medical examiner for Los Angeles County. This is his conclusion:

"Based on my review and analysis of the autopsy and all statements made by participants to the incident, and all parties who took part in its investigation, it is clear that Carlos Hernandez was stabbed numerous times by the same knife, and the stabbings took place at various sites, beginning in the garden area at least twenty feet from the front door of the structure, once again in the entryway, with the great majority while Hernandez was prone underneath and perpendicular to the long end of the dining room table, and that the time of death was at least one hour before the 911 call to police. Furthermore, several more wounds were acquired after his death. There is evidence that Hernandez knew his attacker because there were no defensive wounds to his arms or hands. There is also evidence that Hernandez was helped to enter the mansion or that he was taken inside without his assistance. It is clear that he fell once outside, got up or was assisted up, and eventually came to be under the dining room table where he died. This was a multi-sequence event and not one where Hernandez acquired his life-ending wounds in one place. The person or persons who stabbed Hernandez did so least 23 times. Of these, the majority were rendered while Hernandez was standing, with the most injurious ones while Hernandez was in a horizontal position.   The analysis of his injuries, the examination of his entire body, and the nature of the injuries to critical internal organs led me to conclude that the account of the first officer on the scene was of greatest value in arriving at the cause of death. The investigations by others, such as the senior police accident investigator, Sergeant Newton, are greatly suspects, leading me to conclude that the event did not occur as described by Benjamin Harding Reynolds."

There is no statute of limitations on murder. A case may be brought years or even decades later. In fact, in one unusual instance, a lawsuit was filed and prosecuted almost a century after the death. That was in England and done to overturn the conviction of an ancestor for inheritance purposes and name the perpetrator of the crime.

What would I do with the material from my investigation? I had choices. I could use it to bring civil suits, wrongful death, and even a suit for slander and intentional interference with contractual relations. But the real aim was to have Reynolds charged with murder by the District Attorney for Los Angeles County. This was an election year, and I didn't know how the candidates would handle the information. I decided to circulate word that I had authored an article on the killing, and I would submit it for publication by the Los Angeles Times. And if the Times didn't pick up, the Pasadena Daily News certainly would.

But it never came to that. Reynolds died within weeks of my completion of the investigation. He did not leave any heirs to his fortune, instead leaving the bulk of his fortune to various foundations. The estate was bequeathed to the city of Pasadena to be operated as a museum.

Did I hasten the death of Reynolds? I doubt it. Still, I like to think that I did make those last days unsettling to him and filled with fear and dread that he might have to face criminal charges for what he did. For a man who seldom felt any emotions toward others, that's enough for me. In the end, this narcissistic man — with enough money and power to view the world through his own distorted lens— finally was brought to the point of having to see it through the eyes of others.

If Reynolds is remembered at all today, it is as an eccentric billionaire and philanthropist who, through his civic largesse, helped Pasadena regain much of its architectural glory of old. Down through the years, he acquired many objects of art, paintings, and other historical pieces, that now are on display for a nominal admission price. He also acquired a curious assortment of friends, such as Fidel Castro and Yasser Arafat, along with a trove of lovers. Possessed of a voracious sexual appetite, he had rumored affairs with many celebrities, including noted gay actors Rock Hudson and Liberace, but also some who were bi such as Walter Pidgeon, Anthony Perkins, and Montgomery Cliff.

Most long-time residents of Pasadena associate Reynolds with the "stabbing." For outsiders, the stately Pasadena mansion that he bequeathed to the city is visited each year by thousands, who tour the stately rooms while guides lavish praise on the late billionaire and his benevolence. But they don't bring up the dark and dangerous sides of him that bordered on psychopathic behavior, and that he engaged in morally reprehensible behavior that might have included murder.

POEMS: A DANCE;
A TUNE

A Dance

There is nothing like a dance,
To take your breath away,
To send your senses soaring,
And allow your heart to play.

You walk up to a dance floor,
And a magical thing occurs,
You are half your age,
And shake off all your cares.

You step and then, return again,
To the joys of the dance;
You glide and sway, and prance away,
To the rhythm of romance.

So take that little journey,
To that polished floor,
To lighten up your life,
And enjoy love's metaphor!

A Tune

I have heard a tune,
playing just inside my heart;
with melody and chorus,
each day I hear it start.

It begins quite plain with violin,
and gains with added strength;
the richness and the power,
of every instrument.

It climbs and soars, then declines,
while keeping a steady beat;
then quickly gains in swiftness,
as the refrain repeats.

In time I have come to know,
each note without a doubt;
this tune inside my head,
except when the tune plays out.

ABOUT THE AUTHOR

John Corral

John is an award-winning author of myster-
ies, thrillers, suspense, legal dramas, and
westerns. He also co-wrote and edited
women's stories of love and life with Tanya
Angel, and contributed and edited poetry
with Ian Lewis and Iris Mede.

Books by the author include SERIAL SINS OF
SIBERIA, LUST, LIES, AND LOVE, GETTING
SADDAM'S GOLD, LOVE TIMES ELEVEN,
THE GRISLY EFFECTS OF GREEN, DID
HOLLYWOOD CAUSE THE CUBAN MISSILE
CRISIS?, HIS FINAL RESTING PLACE: ELVIS, REDHEADS ARE
RELENTLESS, DELPHINA: VOODOO QUEEN, 30 FLASHES OF FIC-
TION, 15 FLASHES OF FICTION, 15 MORE FLASHES OF FIC-
TION, MYSTERY AND MALICE, IMPERFECT KILLING, PROSECU-
TION MISCONDUCT, REMEMBERING DIXIE, BEYOND THERE BE
DRAGONS and THE MOST DANGEROUS MAN IN THE WORLD.

Books with Tanya Angel include THE SECRET LIVES OF SMILES,
THE DUCHESS, WHERE THE HEART IS, and WHEN THE HEART
LAUGHS IT SHOW AND WHEN IT DOESN'T IT SHOWS EVEN
MORE.

Books with Ian Lewis and Iris Mede include FLOWING LIQUID
LIFE, DREAMS OF A PERPETUAL DREAMER, EVOLVING LOVE, LET

LOVE FLOAT, ORDINARY LIVES EXTRAORDINARY LOVES, LET LOVE LEAD THE WAY, REAL PASSIONS REAL LOVE, LOVE THAT CHANGES EVERYTHING, THE SENSE OF SORROWS PAST, LOVE DEVILISH LOVE DIVINE, TALKING DIRTY ABOUT DESIRE, LOVE WORTH REMEMBERING, THE PLEASURES AND PAIN OF LOVE, WHEN LOVE LIFTS YOU HIGH, and WHEN LOVE SIZZLES.

John is also the author of TWO BROTHERS, a western, 3 LIFE LESSONS, an essay, and SEEING YOU, a book of poetry.

BOOKS BY THIS AUTHOR

Black Oaks: A Ghost Story

Do you believe in ghosts? Doesn't everyone? I certainly do based on my own experience. This novel was inspired by real events, accounts of ghosts recorded by others, and that happened to me. It is part fact and fiction; the thin line of truth between the two unidentifiable. Is this proof of an afterlife? Perhaps. There is a reason why ghost stories in classic literature are so plentiful. They are meant to comfort, as well as to instill fear. For many, encounters with the unknown are not fiction. Sometimes these encounters take the form of a reunion with a deceased loved one or a confrontation with a strange creature. Scariest of all, our inner demons may haunt us in our most troubled times. No matter how they manifest, paranormal encounters are very real for those who experience them.

The Colors Of Love, Life And Death: And Other Short Fiction

This book of short stories provides a range of topics and characters that have the thread of these three aspects: Love, Life, and Death. Some present love as its main topic, in its many forms; still other detail the harsh realities of life that include death. The eight short stories offer a detailed glimpse of these and transport the reader to other places and other lives presenting life lessons as well.

Two Pandemic Deaths: And Other Stories Of Love And Loss

The story that begins this collection of short fiction pieces is not true. Well, it is not entirely untrue. It was written after the loss of a dear friend, to whom it is dedicated. The sentiments expressed there are also, to some degree, present in the other stories offered here. They were written in somewhat the same melancholy mood. But let that not deter you. For great loss, there must have been great love first, that expands and fills the heart and then breaks the very thing it filled, leaving a hole that may never be fixed.

Serial Sins Of Siberia: And Other Stories

The title selection in this book of short stories, Serial Sins of Siberia, concerns Russia; as does a second, Cold War Comrades: Greene and Philby. But the other five stories do not. And they differ in length, subject matter, genre, and theme. The only thing that binds them together is that they are not boring. Each is memorable and unique in its own way. And though it may seem as if they are non-fiction, given the first-person point of the narrative for some, they are not.

They take the reader from the streets of Los Angeles to the work camps of Siberia, from the notes of a CIA operative to the musing of a retiring attorney. They describe a joyful, complex, ever-changing relationships between a renown writer and a British spy, a lawyer and a porn star; the inner thoughts an avid skier, as well as the whimsical wording of a sale ad for law books; a woman confides in the reader a family secret, and you'll learn of a place where you can be either married and divorced, though not both on your same visit. Each piece showcases different views of life, and differences in individuals. Enjoy!

Lust, Lies And Love: Twenty Tales Of Love Gone Bad

These are stories about love. Not love that is sweet and tender, sublime and true, and has as little in common with reality as unicorns playing in a garden. Things don't always go as people want them to, and, in particular, when it comes to love. A lot of bad things happen instead, things that people may be ashamed of, or worse.

But there is also love in these stories. Some of them, anyway. There is the love of long-term couples, there is the love of newly discovered lovers, and there is the love of friends. There is affection —between lovers, between colleagues, between strangers encountered on the street. There is respect: for love, for desire, for scars, for the complicated places where love and desire overlap. Above all, there is respect for love itself. That to strive for love, and have it —even for a moment, is reason enough to continue to seek it.

Getting Saddam's Gold: And Other Short Fiction

The short stories in this collection were written over the last decade. One appeared in an obscure anthology, another was published in an online magazine, and the remainder are new and original to this anthology. All of them are primarily adventure stories. That is, character and theme are incidental to the plot. Things happen, as opposed to a piece that is a character study or where some idea or interpretation of events is paramount. The object was to tell a good story —unusual and interesting, hopefully, and not moralize about its significance.

Love Times Eleven: A Bittersweet Collection Of Stories

This is a collection of stories about love, in many aspects, in many lengths, and in many forms. The only unifying thread to these stories is the intense emotion of love. But, as you will learn, that may occur in a variety of ways as shown by these eleven separate stories involving a wide variety of individuals, many of whom are shown to be interlinked as the tales progress.

Did Hollywood Cause The Cuban Missle Crisis? And Other Alternative History Stories

These stories are historical fiction. Some are satire and others profoundly serious. Yet they are all plausibly written with facts and events used as the basis for more speculative narratives and alternative accounts of how history might have played out. They provide probable explanations for events or situations that might otherwise be perplexing. Some may call these conspiracy theories, implying falsification or sinister motives. They are neither. Rather, they are reinterpretations of history.

The Grisley Effects Of Green: And Nineteen Other Flash Fiction Stories

For those who already love flash fiction —exceptionally short stories— this book offers you another opportunity to indulge in your passion. For those just now discovering flash fiction, this book introduces you to a true phenomenon in recent fiction trends.

Stories have been growing shorter and shorter, for decades breaking down the conventions of longer fiction. Why? Because flash fiction captures what longer forms can't.

So what exactly does flash fiction do, or capture? As one writer noted, flash fiction can bring you awareness of a point faster and more deeply felt, then, foregoing any novelistic wind-down, leave you there suspended in that wonderful moment of recognition.

It's been said that flash fiction can do in a page what a novel does in two hundred; and, perhaps more humbly, that flash fiction is as intense as poetry, because readers who like to skip can't skip in a one-page story.

This collection provides the full span of this new phenomenon. The length of the entries ranges from one paragraph to nine pages, and includes several poems. They also vary in genre, from humor to mystery, romance to the macabre. And they can go deep; effectively changing you almost before you know it.

His Final Resting Place: Elvis

This book is both a memoir and a portrait of a man who has been written about by many people. Yet this book is unique in many ways. If the person who tells the story is to be believed, Elvis Presley lived on in spirit after his body was laid to rest.
Who is this person who claims that? Who is Marilou Lipsey, the pseudonym she gave herself? Was she really jessi, the name she said Elvis sometimes used to call her?

'Marilou Lipsey' was a neighbor of mine when I lived in North Hollywood, California in the early Eighties. I learned she had "dated" Elvis, but she never said much more about that. We were casual friends only, and I moved away after a few months. About twenty-five years ago she contacted me after she learned I had written a book and said she had a story to tell me that I could publish, but only after her death. That unfortunate event just occurred and thus I am publishing it now. The following is based on what she told me over the course of several days which she said were true events. You be the judge as to the veracity of her story.

—John Corral